S0-AFZ-570

HANNAH AND THE HORSEMAN AT THE GALLOWS TREE

HANNAH AND THE HORSEMAN AT THE GALLOWS TREE

•

JOHNNY D. BOGGS

AVALON BOOKS
THOMAS BOUREGY AND COMPANY, INC.
401 LAFAYETTE STREET
NEW YORK, NEW YORK 10003

© Copyright 1998 by Johnny D. Boggs
Library of Congress Catalog Card Number: 98-96339
ISBN 0-8034-9320-7

PRINTED IN THE UNITED STATES OF AMERICA
ON ACID-FREE PAPER
BY HADDON CRAFTSMEN, BLOOMSBURG, PENNSYLVANIA

For my sisters, Phylis and Vicki—
with apologies for being the ''perfect'' baby

Chapter One

The stagecoach jostled along the tortuous West Texas road, bounced off a rock and sent Hannah Scott ricocheting off the Concord's walls and hard, uncomfortable bench. When the wagon finally stopped swaying violently on its thoroughbraces, she shook her head and resettled into a position that wasn't comfortable but was as close as she could find. She was glad to have the stagecoach to herself. She'd hate to be flopping around like a brook trout against a bunch of tobacco-chewing, cigar-smoking strangers.

Hannah guessed the coach was near Shafter. The heavy, black leather curtains were pulled down over the windows to keep out the dust and wind, and she didn't feel like peeking outside. That would require moving from her spot and risk being catapulted to the rear bench the next time the stupid jehu ran off the road. Besides, she owned 25 percent of the Argo Stagecoach Company and had ridden this route many times—even driven part of it once—and knew they should be in Shafter soon. At least, that's what she hoped. Shafter was her final destination.

She heard the jehu screaming at the horses and felt the stage pull to a stop, heard the messenger screaming back at the jehu to get this Concord moving. The driver was Dick Cody, a tall, cantankerous old man with narrow blue eyes and a mouthful of tobacco in lieu of teeth. He was loco but knew how to drive a stagecoach, and on a Concord the jehu was captain. The messenger, however, was Pete Belissari, a Greek-American mustanger who owned another 25 percent of the Argo and carried a double-barreled shotgun. Hannah heard the squeak of the brake lever being pulled back and knew that Cody had won the argument for now.

"Don't that beat all?" Cody was saying. "Been a long time since I seen somethin' like this."

Belissari spit out a string of profanities. Cody didn't seem to hear him. "Wisht we gots here a tad sooner," he said.

Hannah opened the door and stepped outside, glad to feel hard earth under her feet once more. The Concord was parked in front of Cibolo Creek, which ran through the booming town of Shafter. She could see the Presidio Mine and the ore reduction mill. Behind her was the Men's Clubhouse where single miners lived. People moved around like ants in the busy community. The stagecoach, however, was not supposed to stop until it reached Shafter Station on the south side of town.

Pete Belissari swore again when Hannah stepped outside. He glared at Cody, stuck his shotgun in the boot, and leaped off the driver's box beside her. She looked at the creek, finally realizing why Dick Cody had stopped the stagecoach, why Pete was so upset. A giant cottonwood, its leaves ablaze in bright yellow, grew on the banks of Cibolo Creek, towering over the other scrub brush, mesquite trees, and adobe cottages.

Hanging from one of the cottonwood's massive branches was a man.

His gray eyes seemed to lock on her, though Hannah knew that was impossible. The hangman's noose had seen to that. The black mask that once covered his face had fallen off, or was snatched off, and lay snagged on a piece of driftwood on the edge of the creek. His weight had stretched the rope so now his black boots dipped in the water. His body swayed in the wind, but his eyes never left Hannah.

He was a young man, Hannah guessed, about Pete's age, late twenties or early thirties, with short black hair, a week's worth of beard, hands bound behind his back. He wore a dirty white shirt and gray trousers, and someone had pinned a sign on his chest. Written in a huge, sloppy scrawl:

> *Shafter Does*
> *NOT Tolerate*
> *Murderers*
> *and Thieves*

''Oh, my,'' she said.

Pete turned her away, helped her inside the stagecoach, closed the door, and climbed back into the driver's box. The brake was released, Cody's whip popped, and the Concord splashed across the creek. In a few minutes, the stagecoach stopped again. Belissari opened the door, took Hannah's hand, and led her inside the adobe shack. He offered her a drink. She downed it quickly, thinking it was water, but it was brandy and it burned her throat and detonated like a blasting cap before hitting her stomach. She coughed.

"You all right, Hannah?" Pete asked.

She nodded. "I've just never seen anything like that," she said after a minute. "Get the horses, Pete. I'll be fine."

Pete and Hannah reined up in front of the adobe building near the cemetery. Town Marshal read a shingle hanging above the door, and a woman in a black dress and matching hat stood outside preaching like an evangelist to a timid-looking man wearing a five-pointed tin star stamped Deputy Marshal.

"They made him watch, Mr. Keegan!" the lady yelled. "Do you understand what those two wicked fiends did to my Paulie? They made him watch that horrible display of justice!"

"Yes'm," the deputy said softly.

"Paulie is only seven years old, Mr. Keegan!"

"Yes'm."

"Is that all you have to say, sir?"

Keegan blinked. "Ma'am," he finally answered. "Paulie should have kept his eyes shut."

"His eyes were shut! He was crying the whole time!"

"I heard him."

"Those brutes tied him up, took him to the creek, told him what was happening—my Paulie screaming the entire time at the top of his lungs—and then they told him it was all over and that he could open his eyes now. And he did—just in time to see the horse slapped and Mr. Wilson hanged!"

"Well, ma'am, those rapscallions are locked up now, and they'll be out of our hair directly."

"Rapscallions! They are the devil incarnate! Good-bye, Mr. Keegan. But trust me: You haven't heard the end of this."

"Yes'm," the deputy said and watched the woman storm away. Keegan then studied Hannah and Pete.

"What can I do for y'all?"

"Is the marshal in?" Hannah asked.

Keegan rolled his eyes. "I'm actin' marshal, I reckon. I'm the deputy at least. Marshal Wilson, well, he ain't with us no more."

"Wilson?" Pete said. "The man hanging from that cottonwood?"

"Yep. Marshal's salary wasn't enough, I reckon. He tried to steal some silver, killed a guard, got caught."

"So they lynched him." Hannah's voice was bitter.

Keegan shook his head. "He was tried and convicted, sentenced to hang in Marfa. But I reckon the folks didn't want Marfa to steal the fun, so they came in and took him to the gallows tree."

"And you let them." Hannah was far from sympathetic.

"Ma'am," Keegan said, "I get paid twenty-five dollars a month and free room and board in a jail cell if it ain't filled. I ain't about to risk my neck for no man that a mob of people—people that pay my salary, mind you—are bound to see strung up. Especially a man that's been sentenced to hang anyway. Now you want to file a complaint, you can follow Mrs. Joyner to see Charles Smythe of the Town Council. But he was the fella who slapped the horse and sent Marshal Wilson to eternity."

Pete slid from the saddle, and Hannah did the same. "Actually, Deputy," Belissari said, "we're here to see about the Comhghall twins."

The deputy smiled. "Oh, then you'd be Miss Scott from the orphanage up 'round Fort Davis. Well, why didn't y'all say so? I'm Ulick Keegan. Tie up your horses and step inside."

They followed Keegan into the dark office, where the deputy sorted through a stack of papers at his desk and motioned for his visitors to sit on the bench in front of him. It wasn't much of a bench, only a two-by-six plank stretched across a couple of adobe blocks.

"Y'all got my telegram," Keegan said.

"Obviously," Hannah replied, but the deputy didn't seem to notice her foul mood.

"I didn't really know what to do," Keegan said. "After it happened, we let the kids stay with various folks: Buster Chase, he's a miner, and Mr. Smythe, some others. Now I got 'em. I wired the county sheriff shortly after it happened, and he suggested I get with you. I'm tickled y'all finally come. It was sure something."

"It" had been another murder. Hannah had read about it in *The Presidio County News* long before Keegan's wire arrived. Daniel Comhghall had arrived in Shafter in August, toting along two eleven-year-old twins, a boy named Desmond and a girl named Darcy, and went to work prospecting for another silver strike. His wife, he informed the town, had drowned in the Ben Ficklin flood of '82. In September, Comhghall left Shafter. He said he thought he could find a better living to raise his children in Marfa, which in July had replaced Fort Davis as the Presidio County seat in an election. Passersby found Comhghall's body on the road a short distance out of town. He had been shotgunned to death. Desmond and Darcy were discovered a day later, cowering behind Elephant Rock. The murder of Daniel Comhghall had not been solved.

Keegan scribbled on a form for a minute. He chewed on his pencil, looked at the paper, and returned to writing. "It's Desmond," he said, "and Darcy, and, gosh, that name gives me fits."

"C-o-m-h-g-h-a-l-l," Belissari said. "It's Irish. Pronounced *Cow*all."

"Yeah, well I wished they'd spell it like it sounds. Ulick Keegan's Irish too, or so my pa told me, and it ain't that hard to write." He scribbled some more, slid the piece of paper and pencil to the edge of his desk, and looked at Hannah.

"I reckon you'd better sign this. Paperwork and all." She glanced at the paper. It was a receipt.

"These are children," she said, "not a team of horses."

"Yes'm."

She shook her head and signed the form. Keegan smiled and stuck the receipt in the top drawer to the desk. "How long will y'all be staying in Shafter?" he asked.

"Just today," Pete answered. "We'll take the stage back tomorrow morning."

Keegan nodded. He scratched his head. "I reckon I ought to go ask Mr. Smythe if I can cut down Marshal Wilson's body and bury him. Good thing the turkey vultures is gone for the winter."

"Deputy Keegan?" Hannah asked. He stared at her blankly.

"The children?"

"Yes'm."

"Where are they?"

"Oh!" Keegan laughed at himself. He grabbed a ring of keys off a peg on the wall and walked across the room, unlocked the door, and motioned toward the jail cells. "I'll fetch 'em for y'all."

Hannah shot up, stepped over the bench and screamed at the lawman furiously. "In jail! You left two orphan children in jail? After all they've been through? Locked up with the swine who made that poor little boy watch that lynching! What kind of town is this?"

Keegan swallowed. Belissari waited quietly, not wanting to speak and risk Hannah's wrath turning on him. The deputy scratched his head again. He looked at Hannah and slowly explained: "Miss Scott, them two *Cow*all kids—they was the ones that kidnapped Paulie Joyner and forced him to see Marshal Wilson swing."

Chapter Two

Darcy Comhghall sat on an overturned oak bucket in one of the four cramped cells in the jail, hazel eyes fixated on a tarantula crawling between the iron bars in the small window overlooking the Shafter cemetery. Her round face was smeared with dirt, and straight light brown hair, parted in the center, hung past her shoulders. She wore a brown flannel outfit with plaited skirt and loose jacket trimmed with white braid, unbleached hose, and button boots.

The arrival of Pete, Hannah, and Ulick Keegan interrupted her concentration on the spider, and she glanced over her shoulder at the guests and smiled politely. Hannah knelt at the door and stared at the girl between the cast-iron bars.

"Hello, Darcy," she said softly. "I'm Hannah Scott, and this is my friend Pete Belissari. Do you mind if I talk to you?"

Darcy shrugged. A quick glance revealed that the tarantula was crawling out the window, so she turned to face Hannah again and sighed.

There were two beds in this cell, on opposite ends, a couple of empty plates and tin cups, the bucket Darcy was perched on, and a brass spittoon in case one or both children developed a tobacco habit. A boy's jacket and shirt lay crumpled in one corner next to a small pair of boots. It was disgusting to see two orphans housed in such conditions, and Hannah vowed that someone would hear about this.

"Where's your brother?" Hannah asked.

The girl's head tilted sideways toward the narrow bunk against the adjoining cell. Underneath a ragged, brown woolen blanket was the squirming form of a small boy.

"He's sick," Darcy said, stifling a yawn.

Hannah straightened and commanded Deputy Keegan to unlock the cell. The heavy keys rattled as he found the right one and twisted it in the lock, which clicked. The door was jerked open, and the three adults rushed inside to the bunk, where Hannah slowly withdrew the cover and gasped.

Desmond Comhghall was the spitting image of his sister—with a giant exception. He was sopping wet with sweat that had soaked the ticking mattress and pillow, and his pale face was covered with a bright rash that spread down to his chest and arms. He opened his hazel eyes and spoke weakly, "Mama, my tummy aches and my head hurts."

Ulick Keegan screamed. He backed into the iron bars, turned and groped his way out of the cell, and fled through the open door into his office, yelling, "Scarlet fever! It's scarlet fever!" His voice faded as he ran outside and sounded the alarm down the streets of Shafter.

Hannah couldn't swallow. Slowly she placed the back of her right hand on Desmond's forehead. "Pete," she whispered, and Belissari moved closer. Her face wrinkled. The boy should be burning up, but he didn't have any fever that she could tell. And when she withdrew her hand, she noticed that the red flush had smeared on the boy's forehead and her hand. Scarlet fever was communicable—but not that fast—and rashes don't smear like . . .

"Rouge," she said.

Desmond Comhghall kicked the blanket off him and jumped up. "Run!" he shouted. "Run, Darcy, run!"

The girl bolted out the door as Pete turned, then Desmond was trying to follow, pushing Hannah onto the floor as he attempted to shoot through Pete's legs. Belissari sidestepped the child and grabbed his britches, jerking him to his feet.

"Boy," Pete began, but he never finished.

Desmond charged him like a bull, burying his head in Pete's unsuspecting stomach and slamming the horseman against the hard bars. The kid was almost out the cell, but Belissari recovered and latched on to a skinny, makeup-covered arm, dragging the screaming kid into the cell. The boy twisted around, and Pete jerked him close.

That was a mistake. Comhghall's heel cracked on Pete's toes. Desmond wasn't wearing boots, but Pete couldn't tell. He yelped, let the kid go, and grabbed his moccasin, hopping around the cell. The boy fell backward and scrambled to his feet, but this time Hannah dived across the floor and caught his left ankle. Pete recovered and saw that this orphan was about to kick Hannah in her face, so he seized the boy's shoulders and jerked him back, flinging him into the other bunk.

"Get out!" Pete yelled, and Hannah crawled out the cell like a frightened toddler.

The boy charged again, but Pete blocked his path. His right hand caught Desmond's face. Desmond's teeth sank into Pete's hand. Pete yelled. Desmond kicked him in the knee. Pete let loose with words that a child shouldn't hear. Desmond, in turn, questioned Belissari's ancestry. Hannah was shocked.

Desmond sneered and prepared for another attack, but Pete, shaking his bleeding right hand, jerked the Colt .45 from his holster with his left and pointed it at the eleven-year-old's face.

"You do it," Belissari said, "and you won't live to be a teenager."

"Pete," Hannah said softly. She knew—at least she thought—that he wouldn't pull the trigger. The gun wasn't even cocked.

The boy spit at Belissari's feet, and slowly Belissari backed his way out of the cell, slammed the door shut, and turned the key the deputy had left in the lock.

Desmond stared at them, panting, his face flushed from the tussle and reddened with smeared makeup. He looked angry, like a caged animal, but Hannah knew he also must be frightened. Belissari shoved the Colt into his holster and stared at Hannah.

"You all right?" he asked.

She nodded. "I'm just thankful he didn't grab your gun," she said. "Someone might have been hurt."

Pete's eyes weren't friendly. He glanced at his bloody hand and limped into Keegan's office without speaking.

Charles Smythe was a tall man with penetrating blue eyes, rectangular face and straight nose. He wore a navy shirt with white paper collar fastened by a gold stud, burgundy cravat, gray woolen vest and trousers, and coat of black broadcloth. Everything about him was neat, except the curly dark hair that hung just over his ears and above his collar. Hannah was mesmerized by his English accent. She could just picture him reading *Great Expectations* to the children in her orphanage.

They were sitting in the marshal's office—Pete, Hannah, Keegan, Mr. Smythe, and a miner named Buster Chase who was everything Smythe wasn't.

Chase was short with big ears and a sunburned face. His hair, black but mostly gray, shot out like cactus spines on his beard but was thin on the sides and bald on top. Tobacco juice stained the front of his muslin shirt, his canvas trousers were patched and repatched, and his boots were old and scuffed.

He looked barely able to support himself. Yet this miner was telling them that he wanted to adopt the Comhghall twins.

Once the panic of scarlet fever had been stopped, Keegan and Belissari organized a search party for Darcy Comhghall, but while the miners were fetching their horses and waiting to see if Milton Faver would bring his bloodhounds, up walked Buster Chase carrying a smiling Darcy on his shoulders, proclaiming to everyone that he was going to take those kids in and raise them good and proper.

"He's drunk," Keegan said.

But Chase was sober.

So here they sat.

"Mr. Chase," Smythe said. "You've never married, never had to care for anything other than a horse or mule. You work for wages for the Presidio Mine. And you're, what, fifty-five?''

"Fifty-three!'' Chase snapped.

"Yes, my apologies. Yet you believe you're capable of caring for two eleven-year-olds, two precious children who have witnessed the horror of losing their mother in a flood and having their father gunned down savagely just outside of town.''

"Look, Smythe,'' Chase said. "I was the one who found them kids. I was the first one who took 'em in after their daddy got hisself killed. You remember that?''

"Yes, indeed,'' Smythe replied, "and I also remember that you brought them to me the next morning.''

"Yep. And you give 'em to the widow Joyner, and she brung up to the Nolans and they dumped them with the marshal. But I want 'em back, and I found 'em first.''

Smythe laughed. "These are children,'' he said. "Orphans. It's not like you have right of discovery for a gold claim.''

Chase pointed a stubby finger at Hannah. "I got more right to them kids than she does. She ain't never laid eyes on 'em till today.''

"She runs an orphanage, Mr. Chase. She's well qualified at taking care of children.''

The miner searched the room, found a spittoon, and sent a glob of brown tobacco juice sailing through the air. Hannah grimaced when the miner missed the cuspidor at Keegan's desk. Chase wiped the back of his arm across his lips. "Why don't we ask them Comhghall kids what they think?''

Hannah sighed. The deputy shrugged and walked

back to the jail cells. In a few minutes, he led Desmond and Darcy into the office. Both children smiled politely.

Desmond had cleaned up quite well, Hannah thought. He wore a sailor suit of brown cottonade, boots, and a straw hat. He glanced nervously at Pete as Keegan herded his sister and him to the desk. Hannah closed her eyes sadly as Desmond's left boot stepped into the fresh tobacco juice puddled next to the spittoon.

Keegan scratched his head, unsure of the next step, so Hannah took charge. "Children—" she began, but Buster cut her off.

"Kids," he said, "would y'all like to come live with ol' Buster Chase?"

"Uncle Buster!" Darcy screamed and dashed into the short miner's lap. Hannah frowned. She had seen Desmond nudge his sister before she shouted and ran to Chase. Something was wrong here, but she didn't know what. Or why.

"That settles it," Chase said, rising.

"No it doesn't," Hannah said. "There's no way you can provide for two children. Not the way I can." She was on her feet now, walking slowly toward the puzzled miner. "I've seen enough of this savage little town, Mr. Chase. You can barely cook, and Deputy Keegan has told me about your taste for whiskey, cards, and loose women. I—"

"You'll get these kids over my dead body, ma'am!"

Hannah was furious. "That," she said, "can be arranged!"

Pete stood up to intervene, but Charles Smythe was

a step ahead. He gripped Hannah's left shoulder and spoke warmly. "Friends, friends," he said. "Let us be civil."

Darcy broke into tears, but Hannah had been around children long enough to tell the crying was fake. Buster Chase patted the girl's head with his filthy right hand. Desmond walked over and grabbed his sister's hand. Hannah pouted.

"I think we should sleep on this," Smythe said. "The children can stay with Mr. Chase tonight, and we'll assess the situation in the morning. If needed, we'll wire Sheriff Slaughter or the district judge. But I think we're all in agreement that the welfare of these children must come first."

Hannah nodded. Smythe patted her shoulder. Buster Chase's head bobbed, and he led his new wards outside.

"You sure you want to stay?" Pete asked.

"I have to," Hannah replied.

They had spent the night at Shafter Station. But they hadn't slept. Hannah had been awake, pacing back and forth across the adobe complex, talking to herself, fuming, keeping Pete and the station hands awake all night. Belissari knew she would stay, and, truthfully, he was glad to get away from her and those Comhghall tornadoes. Hannah wasn't much fun to be around when in a huff. Belissari climbed aboard the Concord beside Dick Cody. "Let me know if you need anything," he said.

She forced a smile. "It'll be fine," she said. "I'm sure this will all work out in a day or so, and I'll take the next stage back home with Desmond and Darcy."

"Great," Pete said. He didn't even bother trying to smile.

Dick Cody cursed, whipped the team, and the stage-coach spun up the road and through town. Pete pulled back his hat and tried to sleep. They were hauling one passenger, a man Pete hadn't even noticed. It should be a quiet ride, he thought, which was why he was surprised when Cody pulled hard on the reins and stopped the stagecoach just a few miles north of town.

Pete saw a man standing on the edge of the road, holding a wad of greenbacks in his left hand. "Payin' customer," Cody said, and Belissari nodded, leaving the Parker shotgun leaning against the front boot.

The man grinned. He was in his early twenties, with blue eyes and blond hair, and wore dark clothes and a heavy mackinaw, though it wasn't that cold. "Thanks for stopping," the man said. His voice was hard German, and he slowly unbuttoned his coat and whipped out a long-barreled Remington .45. The smile was gone. "Move and I kill you."

Two men crawled from the rocks above, and a third led five horses onto the road. The three new men had scarves pulled over their faces, and all brandished re-volvers. Pete glanced at the twelve-gauge resting be-tween him and Cody, but he didn't move for it. Instead, he slowly raised his hands over his heads.

"What's going on out there?" a voice cried from inside the wagon.

"Check inside," the man with the horses ordered. Pete stared at him, guessing that he was the leader. He wore a black bib-front shirt and dark herringbone trou-sers tucked inside stovepipe boots. His hat was non-descriptive, but his revolver was a double-action

British Webley and the gun belt and holster were hand-tooled and studded with conchos. The horses were good stock, strong bay geldings about fifteen hands tall, but he couldn't make out the brands.

One of the men jerked open the door to the stage. "What's the meaning of this?" the passenger shouted. Belissari heard a hard thump and a sharp cry and felt the stagecoach sway as the body collapsed inside the coach. The highwayman slammed the door and walked toward the horses, shaking his head.

"Ain't no one in there, Smith," he said, " 'cept some dude I conked."

Dick Cody grunted. "He's all we's carryin', fellas. Y'all picked the wrong coach to rob. We ain't haulin' no strongbox, no money, not even no mail. Now, y'all step aside and we won't keep y'all no longer."

"Shut up!" the German barked.

The other outlaw swore and shouted to the leader with the Webley. "You said they'd be on the stage-coach, Cochrane. Now what are we supposed to do?"

The man with the Webley screamed out a few choice cusswords himself and jerked the bandanna from his ruddy face. He had reddish brown hair with a mustache and goatee. Pete had seen his likeness on several Wanted posters from Presidio to Fort Stockton.

"What's the use in wearing masks if you fools are gonna call me by my name?" Cochrane Smith shouted.

The men mumbled apologies. The German glanced at the stagecoach and back at Smith. "What do we do now?"

Smith's cold, blue eyes fell on Pete. They would kill them. Pete could tell by the leader's eyes. Belissari lunged for the shotgun, but Cody beat him to it, so Pete tried to stand and draw his Colt. He heard the gunshots, saw Cody's body jerk and topple over the stagecoach, heard the shotgun roar, felt the stagecoach lurch and saw Cochrane Smith pull the Webley's trigger just as Pete cocked his revolver.

Belissari's head exploded and he fell on top of the stagecoach and let the blackness cover him like a shroud.

Chapter Three

She found herself walking through Shafter later that morning, stopping to stare at a window display in a store. On a wooden hanger was a dress made of white India linen with narrow embroidery of silk twist, trimmed with lace and satin ribbons. It was, undoubtedly, the most beautiful dress she had ever seen—something she never would have expected to find in a town like Shafter.

"It would look fetching on you," someone said. If she closed her eyes, she could picture Sydney Carton saying those words, or David Copperfield, or Pip Pirrip, or even Charles Dickens himself. She saw Charles Smythe's reflection in the window and smiled at him before turning around.

"At seventeen dollars," she said, "it'll be staying in the store."

Smythe shook his head sadly. "A waste," he said. "A hanger in a dusty window does not do this glorious garment justice, but on you, dear Miss Scott, it would shine like silver." He took her hand and gently kissed it. And bowing, his blue eyes locked on her, he quoted poetry before releasing her hand:

. . . For if my verse can give
Eternity your fame shall ever live,
Fixed as the Capitol's foundation lies,
And spread wher'er the Roman eagle flies.

"Shakespeare?" Hannah guessed.

"John Dryden," Smythe answered and straightened. "I trust you slept well."

"Not at all," she said, and dropped the small talk to get to business. "Have you heard from Buster Chase?"

"No, but give him time. I expect that by tomorrow morn he will be glad to turn those children over to you. Where is your companion, Mr. Be—"

"Belissari. He left for Fort Davis this morning."

"Then you'll do me the honor of dining with me," he said, offering his arm. "I know this quaint little place just a block from here."

He was impeccably dressed from silk bell crown hat to oxford shoes, and wore a linen duster to protect his blue Prince Albert suit. Smythe escorted Hannah to a Mexican café across from the Men's Clubhouse, found a corner table, and ordered coffee, tamales, and tea.

They chatted about the fall weather, the silver mine, and other less important topics until Smythe asked about the orphanage. She told him about the children— Chris, Paco, Bruce, Angelica, and Cynthia—about her involvement in the Argo Stagecoach Company and her place near Wild Rose Pass just north of Fort Davis. Smythe sipped his tea and stared at her without blinking or speaking until she had talked herself out.

"My, Miss Scott—"

"Call me Hannah."

"Hannah. I love that name. You own a ranch, run an orphanage and stagecoach line. You're a remarkable woman. And where does Mr. Belissari fit in?"

"Pete?" She smiled. "I'm his *filenádha*. That's Greek."

"For girlfriend," Smythe said with a trace of disappointment.

"Yes, I know."

Hannah was impressed. "You speak Greek?"

"Ne," he answered. "And French: *Voilà comme je suis.* And German: *Haben Sie ihn gern?* And, if you promise not to tell my father, Irish: *Nochtann gra' gnaoi.* I'm afraid I've forgotten most of the Latin I learned, but I am picking up Spanish living this close to Mexico." He started to say something in Spanish but faltered. "I'm sorry," he said. "I guess I was showing off. Forgive me."

"It's quite all right," Hannah said. "What did you say?"

Smythe shrugged. "I haven't the foggiest," he answered, but Hannah knew he was lying. Still, she didn't push him. Instead, she asked him for his life story.

"Let's see. I attended Oxford University at my father's behest—until I was expelled. And then I joined the French Foreign Legion, again urged by my father, which is where I learned Greek and forgot Latin. A few years later I was back in Coventry before sailing to Dublin and serving on an Irish ship to Galveston. I spent six months on the Texas coast, a year in San Antonio, and several months in New Mexico Territory before I read about your silver strike and decided to visit Shafter. I've been here for six months, and must say I am impressed. At thirty-one, I think I'm finally in my element. The people love me, accept me for who I am. I've read *The Pickwick Papers* and *Le Morte d'Arthur* to crowds at the saloons, and serve on the Town Council. I think I've found a home. This Texas of yours, this Big Bend country, is really quite invigorating.''

''Why did you leave England?''

He finished his tea. ''Again, I owe it all to my father. We reached an understanding after a delicate situation that I would receive a certain stipend from him as long as I kept my 'vile head'—his words, not mine—out of bloody England. I think you Yanks refer to my kind as a 'remittance man.' ''

They were quiet. Neither had touched the tamales, now cold and still wrapped in corn husks. The waitress refilled Hannah's coffee and Smythe's tea. Hannah suddenly remembered Deputy Keegan telling her that Charles Smythe *was ''the fella who slapped the horse and sent Marshal Wilson to eternity.''* This handsome man with the charming manners and wonderful accent, this man who read Dickens and Mallory to miners and quoted Dryden to her in the middle of a dusty boardwalk, had also led a lynch mob, then let the dead body swing for days. Smythe smiled again and unwrapped his tamale. ''These really are quite good, Hannah,'' he said, ''even cold. You really should try yours.''

But Hannah Scott wasn't hungry.

Smythe asked if she would need an escort for the rest of the day, but Hannah declined and the Englishman kissed her hand and walked to the Men's Clubhouse, where Hannah assumed he stayed. She spent the rest of the afternoon meandering around town, casually asking where Buster Chase lived. Some of the miners' homes were nothing but caves in the foothills of the southern Chinati Mountains. Others lived in crumbling adobe *jacals,* and a few had rickety stone shacks.

Buster Chase, she learned, had a small stone house on a hill overlooking Cibolo Creek and the gallows tree. Hannah waded through the shallow water, glad to see that Deputy Keegan had finally cut down Marshal Wilson and buried him, and sat on a pile of stones looking at the house.

By Shafter standards, it wasn't bad. There were four walls and a chimney, a leather-covered window, and a door made of cottonwood slats. The roof was thatch, unlike some of the primitive shacks covered with wagon tarps or cowhide. But she could practically see through the cracks between the stones, which wouldn't keep out the wind, let alone scorpions or snakes. This was late October, and although the days had been pleasant, the nights were chilly. In a month, maybe sooner—in Texas you never could tell—they would be downright cold.

Hannah didn't see Buster or the Comhghall twins. Chase must be in the Presidio Mine. She had no idea where Desmond and Darcy were. They definitely weren't in school; Shafter had no school. If touring the town did anything, it strengthened Hannah's resolve to take those wayward children with her to Wild Rose Pass. It would be a challenge, Hannah knew, because Desmond and Darcy were as wild as Pete's mustangs, but this had to be done. Especially when a miner informed her that Desmond Comhghall had stolen the rouge he used to fake his scarlet fever from Renee's Palace of Sin.

Instead of going to Shafter Station for supper, Hannah decided to visit the marshal's office. Maybe the children had already been returned. She opened the door, but no one was there. Just to make sure, Hannah checked the jail cells, but found them empty. The sun was sinking and the wind picked up, so Hannah helped herself to a cup of coffee, made herself comfortable, and waited.

She must have fallen asleep, because she jumped, spilling the coffee onto the floor, as someone pounded on the door. It was dark outside. She brushed back her hair and walked to the door, which flew open. Hannah recognized the small form in front of her.

"Help!" Darcy Comhghall screamed. "Help! Please help!"

Hannah rushed to the child, whose tears streamed down her face like a waterfall. "What's the matter, Darcy?" Hannah asked.

"He'll kill him, miss! You just gotta help me! Hurry. Please!"

Hannah shook her head, not understanding. "Who'll kill who, Darcy? What's going on?"

"He's beating Desmond, miss. He's gonna beat him until Des tells him where that gold's hidden. Please. We ain't got much time!"

The girl turned and leaped into the darkness. Hannah wasn't sure what was going on. Gold? What gold? But Darcy was running in the direction of Cibolo Creek, and Hannah had a pretty good idea who was beating Desmond. She took off after the girl, who led her right to Buster Chase's front door.

Johnny D. Boggs

A blue enamel lantern hung from a hook on a mesquite post, and light shown from the cracks in the walls. Hannah smelled chimney smoke, but inside the house was quiet. Darcy stepped aside as Hannah ran to the door and immediately began pounding. The latch string was pulled inside, meaning somebody was home.

"Mr. Chase!" Hannah shouted. "Open this door! Open it right now!" There was no reply. Darcy began to cry again. Hannah kicked the door and screamed. "Open up! If you've harmed that child, I'll see you're put in prison! Now open up."

Silence answered again.

Fuming, Hannah stepped back, hiked up her skirt, and kicked the cottonwood door with her two-dollar, canvas-laced shoes. The door creaked, and dust flew from the frame and into her eyes. She kicked again. "Open the door!" she yelled, and jacked her skirt up even higher and slammed her right foot against the hard wood, letting out a silly shriek when the door gave way and sent her falling onto Buster Chase's rocky porch.

She moaned and slowly stood, staring inside. She heard something and saw the figure sway toward her. Hannah took a deep breath and prepared to let the miner have it. He was obviously drunk. She stepped up to face Chase, who staggered into the doorway, reached out, and gripped Hannah's shoulders with both hands.

Darcy Comhghall screamed and fled into the darkness.

Hannah stared at Chase. The man's eyes were glassy, and the glow of the lantern gave him a jaundiced appearance. His lips trembled and he tried to speak. Hannah wanted to step back, but his grip was hard, bruising.

"Mr. Chase," Hannah said deliberately, ignoring the pain, "where is Desmond?"

Buster Chase groaned and toppled forward. Hannah yelled as the short miner fell on top of her. The rocks bit into her back, and something hard and cold punched her stomach. She groaned, sucked in air, and tried to push the drunken fool off her. They rolled over and Hannah climbed on her knees. Chase stared up at her. Hannah checked her stomach, then saw her hands and brought them closer to her face. They were covered in blood.

She looked back at the miner. His muslin shirt was crimson, and buried beneath his ribs was a bone-handled Manasses dirk, which is what had jabbed Hannah's stomach when Chase fell on top of her. The man's eyes bored through her, and she recognized the gaze. It was the same look she had seen on Marshal Wilson, swinging from the gallows tree.

Buster Chase was dead.

Hannah backed away in horror. She looked for Darcy, but the girl was gone. *Desmond!* The thought sent her struggling to her feet and stepping over the miner's body and into the house. "Desmond?" she asked, fearing the worst. There were only two rooms in the house, and Desmond Comhghall was in neither. The leather curtain in the window had been pushed out. If Desmond had been inside, he had fled through here. So had the killer. She briefly wondered if Desmond had killed Mr. Chase but put the idea aside. It would have been self-defense, if Chase were beating him, but no eleven-year-old boy was capable of this: unlocking a folding knife and burying it to the hilt in a man's ribs, then fleeing through a small window. Which meant, Hannah thought, that the killer would be after Desmond—and maybe even Darcy.

She sprinted outside, but tripped over Chase's legs and found herself sprawling on the rugged ground again. She tried to find her feet, but a hand grabbed her shoulder and jerked her back. A scream sliced through the night. Seconds passed before she realized it was her yelling. Hannah closed her eyes, expecting to be murdered, but when nothing happened she looked up to see Deputy Marshal Ulick Keegan staring at her.

"Ma'am," he said, "you're under arrest. You done kilt poor old Buster."

Chapter Four

Just opening his eyes hurt. Staring back at him were a million stars in a cloudless night sky. He smelled mesquite smoke and heard the crackling of a fire and, if he were not hallucinating, someone humming *Oh, Dem Golden Slippers.* Belissari's head throbbed, but he slid himself into a seated position, leaning against a boulder. That was a mistake. His stomach capsized, and Pete thought he was about to lose his breakfast—if he hadn't already.

"Great guns!" a voice boomed. "You're awake!"

Belissari closed his eyes and waited until the nausea passed. When he forced the eyelids open again, he couldn't believe what he saw. Kneeling over him was a man with brown hair, thick eyebrows, and a cleft in his chin. The man could have been anywhere between thirty and sixty. He was decked out in a white Stetson with a five-inch brim, cathedral-arched black boots that came up past his knees, and pants and shirt of white elkskin, both decorated with colorful porcupine quills and six-inch fringe streaming from the seams.

In his twenty-nine years, Pete Belissari had never seen anything quite like this.

"What . . ." He had to pause for a moment. Just speaking made his head pound. "What happened?"

"Well, sir," the man began in a resonating voice that made Pete quiver. "It was highwaymen, you may recall. One stuck his masked face inside the stagecoach. Alas, I had not the foresight to strap on my lethal six-shooters and had left them in my valise, but when I lunged at this ruffian, he planted his cold, hard instrument of terror on my head, and I fell to the floor with a loud *crash!*" He clapped his hands for emphasis. Pete shuddered. His stomach danced.

"I awoke to find the stagecoach flying furiously through the desert—well, off the road, I assure you—leading us straight to destruction, ruin, and death. Your right hand was dangling over the window, and I knew not whether you breathed. But, at great peril to my person, I opened the door and pulled myself onto the top of the stagecoach. The wind whipped my face, but it refreshed me, gave me new life to see my task complete. I knelt over your cold face, scarlet with warm blood, and felt your breath of life.

"At that moment, however, the team of terrified gray steeds broke loose from their traces, and I knew the stagecoach would crash into a giant pile of boulders that would serve as our tombstones if I did not act immediately. So I picked you up and, with the war cry of my blood brothers, the great Lakota Sioux, I plunged into the emptiness and landed in safety as the vehicle was smashed into splinters on those lethal rocks."

Belissari blinked. He absorbed the man's story slowly. Finally, he asked, "Do you always talk like that?"

"I speak as I write, and write as I speak." He reached inside his shirt and withdrew a beaded, leather pouch. From it he pulled a billfold and extracted a business card, holding it inches from Pete's face. Belissari's eyes tried to focus but couldn't quite make out the gaudy letters.

"You'll have to help me," Pete said.

"Of course, sir. My apologies. You can't read."

"I can't see very well!" he snapped, insulted, and pointed to where Cochrane Smith's bullet had glanced off his head.

"I stand corrected. You're wounded, and I thought for a while that you might perish in this desolate region before I learned your name." He returned the card, billfold and pouch. "The honorable Colonel L. Merryweather Handal, noted scribe of the stage and the outstanding literature of the Beadle's Half Dime Library and the Five Cent Wide Awake Library, sold at your finer mercantiles or by subscription and two dollars and four bits a year." Handal smiled, revealing perfect white teeth. "You've heard of me," he added, "perhaps."

"Actually, I have."

"Really?" Handal said excitedly. "I mean, of course you have. I see it in your face. You're an educated man of exquisite taste, who loves the stories of adventure found in my tales—all based on fact, I assure you."

Belissari smiled. "Well," he said, "I know this seven-year-old who's a big fan of yours, Ned Buntline—"

"Buntline! That scalawag can't write. Do you know what his real name is? Edward Zane Carroll Judson. Now, I ask you: Is that the name of a writer of merit or a bunko artist?"

Pete didn't bother to answer. He decided to change the subject. "Where are we?"

Handal sighed. "That, my newfound friend, I was hoping you could tell me. When I awoke, I pulled myself from the overturned stagecoach and discovered your body near the wreckage. We were in the middle of the desert. There was no road that I could see."

Belissari raised a finger. "I thought you leaped off the runaway coach with me?" He smiled, savoring the look on this blowhard after being caught in a lie. Pete wasn't angry. Writers were supposed to have wild imaginations, especially the hacks who churned out those five-penny dreadfuls.

Nonplussed, the honorable Colonel L. Merryweather Handal continued: "Anyway, fearing that those desperadoes would pursue us, I dragged your body through the desert to these hills, carrying you over my shoulders when I could, hiding in the rocks, moving over treacherous terrain for hours, what seemed like days, until, exhausted, I decided to rest here." He cleared his throat. "I think we're safe, for now, from those murderous outlaws."

"I think," Belissari corrected, "we're lost."

"Surely, you know this area, sir. I—I don't have your name."

"Pete Belissari."

"Belissari! A capital name. Italian, or my name isn't L. Merryweather Handal."

"Greek."

"Greek! Outstanding! Although I make my livelihood writing frontier tales for my avid fans, I have always enjoyed the classics as well as my contemporaries like Dickens, Stevenson, Verne, and James. But

Greek literature I find fascinating. Virgil's *Canterbury Tales* is marvelous, don't you agree?''

Pete paused. He had never met anyone quite like L. Merryweather Handal, and West Texas was full of characters. "Chaucer," he said softly, to ease his headache, "wrote *The Canterbury Tales*, not Virgil. Chaucer wasn't Greek. Neither was Virgil. Homer." Pete swallowed. His stomach rumbled. All of this talking and listening wasn't helping his recovery. "Homer was Greek. *The Odyssey? The Iliad?*"

"Yes, of course. But we digress, though literature is always a marvelous topic, and stimulating. As I said, surely you know this area?"

Pete nodded. "We'll see come daylight." He thought about Dick Cody, wondered if the old jehu was still alive. A posse would be looking for them now. The Mexican family at Cienega Station would have become worried and sent someone to Shafter when the stagecoach was an hour or two late. And he doubted if Handal could have carried him far from the wrecked stagecoach. He wasn't worried, but he knew Hannah would be.

Silence didn't last long. Handal snorted and said, "Well, Peter, I can't offer you anything to eat, for we have no provisions, but for a nightcap I have just the right thing." His right hand disappeared into his left boot top and withdrew an engraved pewter flask. He twisted off the cap, savored the aroma, and held the container under Pete's nostrils. "Milton Faver's magnificent peach brandy, the nectar of the gods."

That did it. Pete gagged, rolled over onto his side, and vomited.

"By jingo!" he heard Handal roar. "You've spoiled my thirst!"

Hannah was thrown into the same cell where the Comhghall twins had been held. She found it hard to believe that this dimwit deputy thought her capable of murder. Her protests and pleas did no good. Keegan wasn't even listening. He locked the door and hurried into the adjoining room. She heard him muttering as he left the office and walked toward the red-light district. Hannah's head hurt, so she dropped onto a cot and massaged her temples. The bed was still wet from when Desmond emptied the bucket to make it seem that he was sweating up a storm. She was in jail for murder—Pete would never let her hear the end of this after everything was straightened out—but she was concerned for Desmond and Darcy. They were out in the night, alone, and so was a killer.

Twenty minutes later, the outer door opened and Charles Smythe followed Ulick Keegan into the jail. The Englishman asked to be left alone with her, and the deputy obliged. Smythe grasped the bars with both hands and whispered, "Hannah, what happened?"

She told him all she knew. His eyes never left her, shaking and nodding in all the right places, gasping when she described the death of Buster Chase. When Hannah was finished, Smythe bowed and stifled a cry. She wasn't sure what he was thinking.

"You don't believe I . . . I . . . killed him . . . do you?"

Smythe rose slowly. "No, dear. Certainly not. But you have to realize how this bloody looks." His voice rose excitedly. "Yesterday, Buster Chase said you'd have to take those twins over his dead body. You replied, 'That can be arranged.' And witnesses say they heard you screaming in front of his house tonight. Deputy Keegan found you fleeing the scene, your hands and clothes covered with blood.''

Hannah swallowed. Her hands, skirt, and blouse were still stained red. She hadn't really understood the seriousness of her situation, but the Comhghall twins were her first concern. ''Have they found Desmond and Darcy?''

''No. Ulick's organizing a search party. Listen, Hannah, everything will work out. I promise you. Is there anything I can do for you? Wire your Greek friend in Fort Davis? Have you a lawyer?''

She tried to think. Pete would come as soon as the wire was delivered from Fort Davis to the ranch. A couple of lawyers lived in Fort Davis, but she knew nothing about them. The Tenth Cavalry had transferred out of Fort Davis in April, so the soldiers she had befriended—Colonel Grierson, Captain Leslie, and Sergeant Major Cadwallader—were now stationed at Whipple Barracks in Arizona Territory. Her neighboring rancher, Julian Cale, was trailing cattle to Nebraska. Argo Stagecoach Company president Dean Everhart was in Memphis, Tennessee, visiting his sick mother. Friend and partner Buddy Pecos had been deputized by Presidio County Sheriff Tyler Slaughter to escort two bank robbers to Huntsville Prison. The sheriff? ''Slick'' Slaughter would probably like to see her hanged or shot trying to escape. There was only Pete.

Hannah nodded. ''Please. Wire Pete and tell him what has happened. And tell the Reverend Cox—he's watching over the children—not to worry and not to tell them what's happened. There's no need to get the children all worked up.''

''Anything else?''

''No,'' she said sadly.

Smythe smiled. ''Hannah, trust me. Everything will work out. We'll find this cowardly killer. Right will prevail. It always does. I'll go wake up the bloody telegraph operator.''

And just like that, he was gone. Hannah was alone again. She moved to the other bunk and sighed. Outside, music played from the saloons, people talked excitedly in the streets, dogs barked and horse hooves clopped. She fell back and put her right forearm over her head and closed her eyes. Immediately, she saw Marshal Wilson swinging from the cottonwood limp. Hannah jumped up.

After a few minutes, she heard a door open and a chorus of men's voices, though she couldn't understand many words. Keegan shouted, ''What?'' and let loose with a string of oaths. The cacophony continued. ''What?'' Keegan yelled again. There were more shouts, a couple of grunts, and the scuffling of boots. Next the door slammed. Keegan was mumbling something, then he stomped into the jail while shoving shotgun shells into his canvas jacket.

''This county's goin' up in flames,'' Keegan said, staring at her. ''I got a dead miner, two kids missin' and maybe kilt, and a lady-murderer in my jail—''

''I didn't kill him!'' Hannah argued.

''I caught you red-handed,'' Keegan said, ''and now I got a missin' stagecoach and some other dead folks. I gotta go up the road, so I ain't gonna be here if you need somethin'.''

Hannah screamed at his back. ''Deputy! What missing stagecoach? What dead people? Answer me! Keegan, don't leave. What are you talking about? Keegan? Keegan, come back here!''

The door closed.

''Keegan!''

Hannah kicked the iron bars and cried out in pain, grabbing her right shoe and hopping back to the bunk.

Chapter Five

A night's rest hadn't helped Pete Belissari. The knot on his head still felt like a walnut and was crusted with blood. He tested it gently with his fingers, flinching at the pain, and pulled himself up, using the boulder for support, studying the pockmarked terrain while listening to Handal's snores. A canyon cut into a terraced mesa in front of him, flanked by scrub oaks and sotol stalks. Higher up he could make out juniper and madrone. Behind him stretched the desert flats.

Dizziness sent him sliding to a seated position. He sighed. His holster was empty and his hat gone. He couldn't wear the hat—not the way his head felt—but he sure wished he had that .45. The search party looking for him would hear the shot. Then again, he thought, so might Cochrane Smith if he were still in the area.

The snoring stopped. For a second, Pete wondered if the writer had quit breathing, but Handal yawned and rose, found his flask, and sipped his peach brandy. "By jingo," he said, his voice reverberating like an Army sergeant barking out orders. "I could use some coffee this morning, a half-dozen eggs, a stack of flapjacks, and a side of bacon. How are you feeling this grand day, Paul?"

"Pete," Belissari corrected. "I'm tolerable."

"Have you established our position, lad?"

He nodded toward the canyon. "I think," he said, "if we head in that direction we should come to La Morita."

"La Morita?"

Pete pointed at the flask. "One of your friend Milton Faver's ranches. He runs his goat and sheep operation at the springs there."

"Milton Faver, Peter, is no friend of mine. I visited him at El Fortín del Cibolo intending to acquire information for my next writing endeavor. He was gracious at first, but when the old coot realized my purpose, he flung me out by my ear."

"Don Melitón's not as tough as he used to be. Ten years ago, he probably would have shot you, or had you dragged through cactus."

"I thought Faver was strictly a cattleman, trader, and purveyor of fine liquors. Had I known he raised sheep and goats, I never would have visited him, except, maybe, to sample his brandy. Sheep and goats are disgusting animals."

"How does mutton sound?"

Handal smacked his lips. "Of course, mutton would be capital. Simply capital. Perhaps we could also have some beans and tortillas, and maybe they would have a keg of Faver's brandy at La Morita. My flask, it seems, is running low."

Belissari felt nauseated again and closed his eyes. "Let's wait awhile, Mr. Handal. I'm not quite up to walking."

"Certainly, Peter. And, please, call me Colonel."

* * *

Hannah had two visitors that morning. The first was Mrs. Joyner, who came in screaming that her Paulie was sick. "Sick as a skunk," she shouted, "with a high fever!" Hannah had no idea who the woman thought she would find in jail. "Where is that job-simple deputy?"

"I don't know," Hannah said tersely. "Why don't you find a doctor?"

"We have no doctor in Shafter, madam!" she said in a huff. "The nearest one is in Presidio, and I must send Deputy Keegan to fetch him. My Paulie is sick. And so is Mr. McCourt's daughter!" With that, the woman fled the jail, screaming Keegan's name as she ran down the streets.

Ten minutes later, Charles Smythe entered the jail. He was much calmer than Mrs. Joyner. Hannah, on the other hand, felt like raw nerves.

"Charles!" she yelled. "Keegan left last night and said something about a missing stagecoach and more dead people! What's going on?"

Smythe let out a heavy sigh. Hannah thought she might cry, but she bit her lip and braced herself. "It's bad," the Englishman said. "We found that old stage-coach driver by the road, just outside town." Smythe paused. "He's dead, Hannah. Shot to bloody pieces!"

Hannah breathed deeply and slowly exhaled. "And Pete?"

Smythe shook his head. "He wasn't there, and neither was the stagecoach. We don't know where the stage is, Hannah. It's simply disappeared."

There was more, Smythe said. Since the crime oc-curred outside the town limits and therefore was a county matter, Sheriff Slaughter had wired Keegan, appointing him special deputy to investigate. Keegan, in turn, had deputized Smythe. While Keegan rode to Cienega Station, Smythe was to organize a search party to locate the stagecoach or find the killer or killers. The Englishman paused.

"Some people," he said, "think that your friend Pete killed the driver and took the stagecoach."

"Charles, that doesn't make a lick of sense. There was no money on that stagecoach and just one passenger, some dude who looked like he was part of Buffalo Bill's Wild West Show. Why would Pete want to steal a stagecoach—especially when he has a quarter interest in the company?"

"I agree, Hannah. These miners, though, can be peculiar."

Hannah had a million other questions. What had taken them so long to realize the stagecoach was missing? Had they checked the canyons along the route between Shafter and Cienega? Couldn't they follow the tracks left by the stagecoach and team?

"Please, Hannah," Charles said. "I don't know much, and I have to get this search party ready. The wind last night blew away most of the tracks, so I've sent word to the Rangers in Presidio to bring the best tracker they have. We didn't find out what had happened sooner because . . ."

He stopped again, sighed, and continued: "When the stage was two hours late, your man at Perdiz Creek Station sent a rider south to see what was the matter. When he came to Cienega . . . he . . . he found that . . . that poor Mexican family . . . *murdered.*"

Hannah was devastated. The Bautistas were simple sheepherders who ran the station stop for extra money.

She could picture Beatriz and Jorge, their daughter Maribel with her sweet smile, and the two station hands, Vasco and Paolo. Why would anyone want to kill them?

Smythe shook his head as if answering her question. "The rider galloped back to Perdiz to tell his boss what had happened, then he raced here and informed Deputy Keegan. By then it was dark."

For the first time, Hannah noticed Smythe's clothes. Gone were the Prince Albert suit and fancy hat. Instead, he donned high-topped boots, chaps over his trousers, with a gray flannel shirt and dented black Stetson Boss of the Plains. A black leather gun belt was strapped across his waist, with a Colt Lightning, just like the one she had at her ranch, stuck in the holster on his right hip.

"I have to go, Hannah," he said. "Keep your head up, dearest. This will all work out."

Colonel Handal pulled a brass telescope from his boot and scanned the landscape while Pete rested. "Hmmmm," Handal said, "dust." That got Belissari's attention. He struggled to rise and took a tentative step toward the writer. "Great Scott! Riders, Peter, riders. I believe we have been delivered from Death's cold, clammy clutch!" With his right hand, Handal found a small revolver that Pete hadn't noticed.

"Four men," the colonel said, "led by a giant of a man wearing a black sombrero and riding a magnificent white steed." Pete moved quickly now, fighting off dizziness, nausea, and pain. "The others are also Mexicans, I believe, on outstanding horseflesh, traveling fast. They don't see us, Peter, but fear not, lad, this Remington shall alert them of our presence!" Handal tossed the telescope aside and raised the dainty little No. 4 Smoot over his head.

Belissari dived, bringing his right hand across the .38-caliber pocket pistol just as Handal pulled the trigger. The heavy hammer bit into Pete's little finger, preventing the revolver from firing. He yelled in pain and fell hard to the earth. The Remington gripped his hand like a mousetrap, but upon hitting the ground, it jerked the flesh from Pete's knuckle and clattered against the stones.

Pete rolled over, setting his jaw, gripping his bleeding hand, fighting back tears. Handal stared down at him as if he were a fool.

"What was the meaning of this, Peter?" the colonel snapped, and bent to retrieve his revolver.

Belissari brought his left moccasin down firmly on the .38, sat up, and studied his hand. He would have a nice scar, right next to the teeth marks courtesy of Desmond Comhghall. When his breathing was finally under control, he looked up at Handal. "Big Mexican. Black sombrero. White horse. Doesn't that mean anything to you?"

"It means that they're riding away, Peter. They could have rescued us."

"Murdered us," Pete snapped. "That's Plomo."

"Plomo?" Handal spun around and stared at the fading dust. "Plomo! But of course. *Plomo, The Terrible; or, The Masked Rider of Mexico.* I spun that mighty yarn when I was writing for Beadle's in '78. Three years later I jumped to Wide Awake and gave them *Plomo's Revenge; or, Mayhem in Old Monter-rey.* I didn't know the old horse was still kicking.''

"Kicking, shooting, stabbing, and pillaging all along the border for twelve years now." Paco had enjoyed those two books especially, Pete recalled. He handed the Smoot to Handal, wrapped his bandanna around his bleeding hand, and let the colonel pull him to his feet.

"Come on," Pete said, "let's start walking to La Morita."

"Are you sure you're up to it, my friend?"

"I'd better be," Belissari answered.

She lay on the bunk, listening to her stomach growl. She hadn't eaten since noon yesterday with Charles Smythe, and then she had only picked at the tamales. Outside came men's laughter and piano music. A coyote howled, and the chilly night wind blew dust into the cell. Waiting, hoping that someone would bring her something to eat, Hannah drifted off into a dreamless sleep.

The door flew open, and a shrill voice screamed at her to wake up, to hurry, to get moving. Hannah rubbed her eyes and sat up in the bunk. Someone held a lantern in front of the doors. Someone small.

"Hurry!" Darcy Comhghall shouted. Hannah realized that the girl wasn't talking to her. She was yelling into the marshal's office. Shoes scuffled, a chair scraped across the floor, and then Darcy's twin brother ran into the jail, the heavy key ring jingling at his side.

"What are you two doing?" Hannah said, half-asleep, still not comprehending.

"You got to hurry, ma'am!" Darcy yelled. "They're coming for you."

Desmond worked a key into the lock. It didn't fit, so he found another one. Hannah thought she was dreaming.

"Ma'am, trust us," Darcy pleaded. "We don't want to see you hurt."

Hannah came full awake and shook her head. "Stop it," she ordered. "Stop it right now, Desmond. You'll get in a lot of trouble. Put those keys back!"

The boy didn't listen. He went to another key, shoved it in the lock, and twisted it until he heard the heavy metallic click. The twins smiled simultaneously as Desmond pulled the door open with a loud, long squeak.

"Close that door!" Hannah yelled. The Comhghalls didn't obey.

Darcy said, "Hurry, miss! We don't have much time!"

Hannah stepped forward to pull the door to herself, but Desmond moved in front of her and cursed vehemently. It was something she would expect from Buddy Pecos, maybe Pete when he was angry, and herself when the children weren't around—but not from an eleven-year-old.

"Woman!" Desmond snapped. "You better follow us if you don't wanna follow in Marshal Wilson's footsteps!" And he pointed out the window.

She heard the commotion then, realized the music from the saloons had stopped. A dog wailed as if it had been kicked. She could understand the words now. *Buster didn't deserve to die, but she does.* Shouts of agreement followed. Hannah moved hesitantly to the far end of the cell, stepped onto the bunk, and peered through the barred window. They were coming, maybe two dozen men, slugging back whiskey and shouting angrily. Some held torches that illuminated their dirty, bearded faces. A couple toted shotguns.

And one, a big man with a red mustache and vicious scowl, carried a rope.

Chapter Six

This cannot be happening to me, Hannah thought. But it was. She froze, unable to even breathe, at the sight of those men coming to kill her. The Comhghall twins' screams snapped her into movement; she left the damp, cramped cell and followed the two children out of the marshal's office, moving like snakes in the shadows, through the thick creosote bushes and stumbling through the cemetery.

They rested amid the wooden crosses and carved stones, listening. A gunshot rang out from outside the jail, followed by shouts and the ringing of a bell. The would-be lynchers had discovered that she had escaped. A posse would be organized. She knew she would be caught, dragged back to the gallows tree, and murdered. A makeshift tombstone caught her eye. It was a boulder lodged at the head of a rocky mound, with two words scratched on its face:

UNKNOWN
1884

Would her epitaph be similar?

"Now what?" Desmond asked his sister.

"We can't let them catch her," Darcy said.

"They'll string her up like they did that marshal man."

"You liked seeing that."

The girl closed her eyes and shuddered. "Not really. I thought I would, but I didn't. I'm sorry we made that boy watch."

"I ain't. It was funny. And he was a sissy."

"Well, she's your responsibility. But we got to hide."

"Then don't talk so loud. Them men will hear us."

Hannah tried to speak, but couldn't. A coyote wailed in the mountains, and she shivered. The boy said something about heading to the old mine, the girl nodded, and they motioned for Hannah to follow. She didn't think her legs would work, but they did, and she and the twins pushed their way through a fence of sotol stalks, crossed the street, and ducked behind a privy just as two horses galloped by.

They waited for a minute until satisfied the riders hadn't spotted them. Then they inched down the rocky slope to the banks of Cibolo Creek. Desmond waded in, and Darcy grabbed Hannah's right hand and led her into the shallow but cold stream. "They won't be able to track us in water," Darcy whispered, and the three slowly walked upstream toward the hills, stopping occasionally to listen and stealing glances over their shoulders.

Hannah had no idea how long or far they had traveled. Her shoes were waterlogged, and the wind bit her nose, cheeks, and ears. Desmond stopped and brought a finger to his lips. Hannah turned around and listened, but the only sounds were the shrubs rustling in the wind and the rippling of the water over the rocks and their numb ankles. Behind her she made out the flickering lights of Shafter and a few stars where the clouds had broken up.

"I think we're safe," Desmond said after a minute and sloshed his way to the bank. Darcy found a seat on a fallen cottonwood branch, pulled off her shoes, and massaged her feet.

"We ain't got time for that nonsense," the boy said, but Darcy stuck out her tongue and continued trying to get the blood circulating again. Desmond sighed and looked at Hannah, who pried off her shoes and emptied them of water.

"Well, lady," he said, "what do you intend on doing?"

An owl hooted. Darcy started to scream, and her brother shot up. "Quiet!" he ordered. "It ain't nothing but an old hoot owl, so stop acting like a girl! If them fellows find her, it means they find us—and you know what that means!"

Hannah squinted, trying to comprehend. "What does it mean, Desmond?" she asked.

The boy looked at her. "Well, looks like the lady can finally talk again. It means, miss, that after they hang you, we get killed."

"Desmond," Hannah said, "those people won't kill you. And once they've calmed down, they won't kill me. We'll wait until morning, then go back to town." She was thinking clearly now, understanding what she should have done in jail. Running was silly. Stupid! She could have sent the children for Happy Jack McBride and David Goldman at Shafter Station. They would have been able to talk sense into those men, or stop them by force. Or Charles Smythe. He would have been able to reason with them. They would listen to him.

But it was too late now.

"Lady," Desmond said, "we ain't going back to Shafter. It's dangerous."

"That's right," his sister said. "We'd be deader than dirt."

Hannah smiled. "It'll be safe," she said, "I'm sure."

Desmond scoffed and said, "Tell that to Buster Chase."

That stopped Hannah. The children were whispering between themselves now, Desmond arguing that they never should have brought her, Darcy saying that it would be all right, both of them agreeing that they had to go to the mine, then the girl whining that she was tired and cold and wanted to go to sleep. Both stopped and stared at Hannah.

"You sure you want to go back to town?"

She wasn't sure now, but she nodded. If she could get to Happy and Goldy, or Smythe, she'd feel safe. And if she were caught running away, it would be too dangerous for the children. Those men might shoot first before Hannah could surrender, and Desmond and Darcy could be in the line of fire.

The boy sighed. "Well," he said, "I reckon we can sleep here tonight. Like as not, them oafs in town think we'd run south, to Mexico. Then maybe we can talk some sense into your fool head come morning."

Desmond stalked off into the darkness. Hannah hadn't realized how exhausted she was. Darcy came over, and the two curled up next to each other on the uncomfortable ground, warmed only by their body heat. Hannah fell asleep in seconds.

They picked their way up and down the mesa, and Pete pointed to a grove of trees that in the distance appeared as nothing more than a dark spot on the horizon. "El Morito?" Colonel Handal asked.

Pete shook his head. "A camp some miners used before the Shafter strike. I think it's abandoned now, but someone might be using it. Anyway, there's water there, and we can rest for the night. We'll be at La Morita—not El Morito—tomorrow morning."

Handal smiled and resumed his life story. He hadn't shut up since morning, talking his way through thickets and over rocks, occasionally sipping brandy. Pete's throat was dry. He didn't know how the colonel could talk so much.

L. Merryweather Handal was born in 1839—shortly after noon on August 13 to be precise—in Philadelphia. His family moved to Saint Louis in '52, where Handal's father worked as a printer. Handal followed his father into the trade before trying to write, landing a job as a correspondent for a Saint Louis paper. When the War broke out, *Harper's Weekly* turned Handal down but he sent dispatches to various papers in Ohio and Missouri, earning the sobriquet "Colonel" at Wilson's Creek in '61. After Elkhorn Tavern the following year, Handal had seen enough of war so he took a stagecoach west and wound up working as a printer for the *Territorial Enterprise* in Virginia City in the fall of '62.

Pete had gotten just one sentence in when he asked if Handal had known Mark Twain. Belissari had heard that Twain worked for the Nevada newspaper in the '60s.

"Samuel Clemens!" Handal hissed. "That ne'er-do-well! The man's the devil incarnate! I loathe Mark Twain. I had to type that fool's idiotic prose for the *Enterprise*. And then, when I'm in California, they sent him to the Sandwich Islands when I would have gone at half the price and written articles ten times better and more accurate, more exciting. My first novel came out in '75, but what notice do I get? None! Everyone's talking about *Tom Sawyer*. And have you heard of his new book?"

Even if Pete dared to answer, Handal didn't give him enough time. "Scandalous! Simply scandalous. But trust me, Peter, years from now Americans—no, citizens of the world!—will be reading the works of Colonel L. Merryweather Handal, and *The Adventures of Huckleberry Finn* will be long forgotten. Mark Twain indeed! Yes, I know him. And if he were here today, I'd shoot the scamp dead! Now where was I?"

Handal took a deep breath and continued his life story. He set type for the *Call* and *Alta Californian* in San Francisco after leaving Virginia City in '65, then spent eighteen months in the Colorado gold fields before returning to Saint Louis. He married in '69, divorced in '70, married again in '71 and divorced again in '72, and married and divorced in '73 before swearing off women and John Barleycorn forever and taking a job with the New York *Express* in '74. He left the newspaper the following spring with his publication of *The Luck of the Lucky Lady* in DeWitt's Ten Cent Romances.

By the fall of 1875, he was writing steadily for

Beadle's. He penned and produced a play in '78 that opened and closed within a week. In '81 he moved to the Five Cent Wide Awake Library before tragedy struck in '83 when he married again, rediscovered whiskey, and his new wife left him for one of his editors at Wide Awake, who quickly and unceremoniously fired the honorable Colonel L. Merryweather Handal.

"Which, Peter, brings me here," the colonel concluded with a sigh.

Pete enjoyed the silence. He stretched his back and nodded toward the camp, but before he could start walking, Handal was at it again: "Beadle's wouldn't take me back. They say I've lost my touch, say my stories aren't interesting anymore. Bosh! I'll show those swine. So I'm here to soak up the atmosphere, to find something new to write about. I'll show those fools and that shameless hussy I married!"

Handal drained the last drops of brandy and flung his flask into the rocks. He had nursed the liquor an amazingly long time. "Are you married, Peter?" Before Belissari had finished shaking his head, the writer asked. "Have you a girlfriend?"

"I guess so."

"Would you like some advice?"

Pete didn't answer.

"Marry her, Peter. I enjoyed my bachelordom and my abstinence from women after my second, no, third divorce. And even after that worthless petticoat—I found her through a mail-order service, by the way—cost me my job and my apartment in Manhattan, I know now that a man is not whole without a woman.

Shakespeare put it best when he wrote: 'Marriage is honorable in all.' ''

''I think,'' Belissari said, ''that's from the Bible, not the Bard.''

''Oh. Well, come on, my friend. That cabin isn't getting any closer with us just sitting here.''

It took them more than two hours to walk to the cabin. Weak from the loss of blood and lack of water, Pete stumbled to the small spring, cupped his hands, and drank thirstily. Handal did the same. Belissari bathed his head wound with his bandanna, then leaned against a massive cottonwood and studied the cabin a hundred yards away.

''Strange,'' Handal said. ''I didn't realize how thirsty I was. It's not terribly hot.''

''You're in a desert,'' Pete said. ''We're high up in elevation, but you still need to drink a lot of water. There's someone in the cabin.''

Handal glanced at the building. Smoke rose from the chimney, and a door opened. A tall figure carried a bucket (of grain, Pete guessed) to a stone corral that blocked their view of the horses. Handal clapped his hands, rose quickly, and splashed across the spring toward the cabin.

''Excellent!'' the colonel shouted. ''Do you smell that, Peter? It's coffee, biscuits, and bacon. And I, for one, am famished!''

''Colonel!'' Pete cried, but it was too late. He had been about to ask Handal for that silly little pocket pistol he carried. Instead he swore. The man sat the bucket down and stared at half-running Handal and yelled something to the cabin. Belissari thought about sneaking away, just to be safe, but decided against abandoning Handal. He'd take his chances that the cabin dwellers were friendly. Besides, the coffee did smell good.

"We've been waylaid by some vicious highway-men, my friend," Handal was telling the gray-bearded man when Pete caught up. "We have traveled across this most formidable country, an arduous task I assure you, especially since this young messenger was seri-ously injured by those rogues. I hope we may impose on you for some coffee and grub." Handal winked. "And maybe some brandy if you have any, although whiskey will do."

Handal stepped forward and held out his right hand. "I am Colonel L. Merryweather Handal, author and playwright, at your service."

Pete looked at the cabin and sighed. Cochrane Smith walked into the yard, followed by two other outlaws. The gray-bearded man smiled and drew his revolver.

"Well, well, well," Smith said. He didn't stop until he stood face-to-face with Belissari. "Kid," he said, "search Colonel Handal, please."

The blond gunman who had stopped the stagecoach hurried to the flabbergasted Handal. He tossed the tel-escope, beaded pouch, and other items into a pile, and broke into laughter when he discovered the Remington .38, which he handed to the graybeard.

"Here, Baker," the German said. "Give to lady friend in El Paso."

Baker laughed and shoved the Smoot revolver into his waistband.

Cochrane Smith smiled and brushed Pete's hair to the side and examined the wound. "Hmmmm," he said, drawing the Webley and staring at the revolver in his right hand. "Either you got one hard head, *amigo*, or I need to increase my powder load."

Pete said nothing.

"Sir," Handal pleaded. "All we ask of you is some food and water and we'll be on our way. You have our word as gentlemen that no one shall learn of your hideout from us."

"You won't need food where we send you," the German said.

"But they'll sure need water!" Baker slapped his thigh and enjoyed his joke.

"That's a fact," Cochrane Smith said, cocking his revolver and placing the barrel on the bridge of Belissari's nose.

Chapter Seven

"Go ahead," Pete said. "They'll hear the shot."

Smith laughed. "Who? A posse? I ain't a-feared of any milksops Shafter sends out."

"How about Plomo?"

The killer's eyes registered surprise, and maybe fear. The fourth outlaw, a scrawny man shaped like a fence post, said, "He's bluffin', Smith." But the leader was wavering, and Pete was silently praying: *Please, God, let Merryweather Handal be quiet just this once.*

Smith's long finger relaxed against the Webley's trigger. Pete stared at him, though it was difficult with the gun barrel between his eyes. "We would have waited by the stagecoach for the posse," Pete argued calmly, "if we hadn't spotted Plomo." He nodded toward the outlaw Baker. "We would have fired that Remington Smoot as a signal if not for Plomo."

"He speaks the truth, my friend!" Handal interjected. Outwardly Belissari seemed calm; inside he stewed, wanting to strangle that imbecile, wishing the hack had stayed in New York, wishing God had heard his prayer. "I spotted the border ruffian with my telescope. A giant of a man, a full six-foot-six in his stockings, wearing the black sombrero and riding a

57

fantastic white stallion. Why, he was followed by thirty or forty men, all armed with instruments of death. And in case you are not familiar with the treacherous borderman, let me quote, from memory, from my *Plomo, The Terrible,* which my editor at the Beadle's Half Dime Library called my signature work, a classic better than anything Ned Buntline ever dreamed of writing:

" 'All along the Rio Grande from the canyons of southern Texas to the badlands of Arizona Territory, the name Plomo registered fear in the hearts of even the bravest men, women, and children. His black sombrero produced the kind of panic that the pirates's skull and crossbones induced in the days of old. He—' "

"Shut up, you fool!" Baker shouted.

Pete wanted to wet his lips. Baker was scared. The German, however, wasn't. Fuming, the young outlaw walked toward him, drew his Remington in midstride, thumbed back the hammer, and pressed the barrel against Belissari's temple.

"If you scared, I kill him," he told Smith.

Smith holstered his Webley and turned to face his confederate, ordering: "Put it away." As soon as the blond kid shoved the revolver angrily in his holster, Smith slapped him savagely with his backhand. The German staggered back, stunned. Belissari let out a breath.

"You think I'm yellow, Hildebrecht, you question my authority again!" Smith snapped. "I'll kill you where you stand. This is my gang. I run it. If you, Baker, or MacGregor don't like it, leave." He lowered his voice. "Maybe you'll run into Plomo."

"I still say Plomo ain't here," MacGregor argued.

"You want to risk it? Plomo's after the same thing we are."

MacGregor frowned. "Now you didn't say nothin' 'bout no Plomo when I joined up."

"Well, now you know." Cochrane Smith's face flushed with anger, his ears a dark scarlet. "Plomo knows about the gold too! You don't like it, ride out. That goes for all of you numskulls. What we got to do is get them twins before he does. And I ain't riskin' no shot and bring that man-killer to this fandango."

Baker scratched his beard. "Well, if it's the shot you're afraid of, Cochrane, why don't we just slit their throats?"

"Because that ain't my style! A man uses a gun to kill a body, not a knife. A knife . . . a knife is . . . too personal!"

Kid Hildebrecht rubbed the pink spot on his cheek. "Well, what do with them?" he asked.

Smith removed his hat and ran his fingers through his thick hair. After a minute, he said, "Lock them in the smokehouse. That thing's built like a fort. Then we'll light a shuck out of here and get after them kids."

Baker and MacGregor forced Pete and Handal into the small stone building that smelled like mesquite-smoked ham but was empty of food. The door slammed shut, and Belissari heard the click of a heavy padlock. He sat on the floor and leaned against the cold wall, worrying. Handal, meanwhile, scavenged the floor. Pete didn't know what the colonel was looking for. Morsels of food?

The twins, Smith had said. The gang had stopped

the stagecoach outside of Shafter, looking for some-one. The twins. Darcy and Desmond Comhghall some-how were believed to know the whereabouts of gold, and Cochrane Smith and Plomo, two cold-blooded killers, the worst in the Big Bend, were after them.

Hannah would be caught in the middle.

"Aha!" Handal exclaimed and held a bent fork in his right hand. "A tool, my friend. We'll dig our way out of this predicament, much like d'Artagnan in *The Count of Monte Cristo.*"

Pete didn't respond. He didn't bother to point out that they were sitting on solid bedrock. Nor did he tell the colonel that Edmond Dantes was the hero of *The Count of Monte Cristo*, not d'Artagnan, and that it had taken him fourteen years to escape the prison at Château d'If.

Half-asleep, Hannah knew something was wrong when she tried to scratch her nose, and something bit into her wrists. She sat up groggily and, after blinking away sleep, saw the manacles. The screw-locked handcuffs were fastened tight, and a hemp rope had been firmly knotted around the small chain that con-nected the rusty iron cuffs. The rope led from her to a packsaddle on a mule, where Desmond and Darcy were having an animated discussion.

"What do you kids think you're doing?" Hannah shouted. She shook her secured wrists angrily. "Take these handcuffs off me!"

The twins glanced at her briefly, then continued their discussion. Finally, Desmond said, "Fine. You ride," and helped his sister climb aboard the mule. Desmond must have purloined the handcuffs from

Keegan's office; she didn't know where he got the mule. Hannah climbed to her feet, tripping once and cutting her right knee on a rock, and started toward the Comhghalls.

Hannah's fury refused to subside. She'd brain them both with the handcuffs. She whip them with the rope. She'd find the keys and chain those to devils together and drag them down Cibolo Creek with the mule. She'd gouge their eyes out.

Desmond walked to meet her charge, stopped suddenly, and grabbed the rope with both hands and jerked it forward. Caught off guard, Hannah planted her face in the dirt.

"I'll say this just once, lady," the boy said. "I told you we ain't going back to Shafter. Now you're coming with us. We won't hurt you none."

Hannah pushed herself up and spit dirt out of her mouth. She spewed venom at the children, using words she had picked up—but never uttered before— from Buddy Pecos. Her face reddened with anger. She screamed at them. Desmond turned to his sister and muttered, "Told you we should have gagged her."

"Lady," Darcy pleaded. "That posse might hear you. You don't want to hang, do you?"

Right now, she wanted to hang them. But the girl was right. So she shut up, scrambled to her feet, and ran at them silently. Desmond turned and slapped the mule with a shriek, "Get moving, mule! Run!" Hannah had hoped the mule would be stubborn, that it wouldn't budge, but instead he took off at a lively clip. The slack in the rope tightened, Hannah almost lost her footing, and now she had to run to keep from being dragged through the prickly pear and stones.

Desmond sprinted in front of the mule, took the reins, and trotted in front, leading his convoy toward the high country.

Hannah stumbled along behind them, her feet and ankles already aching, her hands numb from the pull of the iron cuffs. They kept this up for about an hour, neither Desmond nor the mule showing any signs of exhaustion. Hannah fell once, and the rocks ripped a gash in her skirt all the way up to her left hip. The mule didn't stop, so Hannah had to pull herself up and keep running. She fell a second time fifteen minutes later, and this time, she couldn't get up. The mule dragged her a good twenty yards before Desmond stopped him.

Hannah's chest heaved, and the cold morning air burned her lungs. She stared into the sun, mouth parched, wondering what was going on, how she had let things get so out of control. Closing her eyes, she tried to think. She was in her mid-twenties, dealt with orphans every day, yet she, in fact, had been kidnapped by two eleven-year-olds.

A shadow crossed her face, and she looked up at Desmond. The kid held a blue enamel cup and offered it to her. Hannah waited until she could control her breathing and slowly sat up. A dizzy spell almost flattened her, but she shook this off and took the cup, brought it to her lips, and tasted the cool, sweet water. Her eyes fell on something swimming in the water and Hannah screamed and splashed the contents on the rocks. A wet scorpion, its stinger waving angrily, disappeared under a smooth stone.

Desmond laughed, took the cup, and filled it again with water.

"Des," his sister said, "what did you do?"

"Put a scorpion in her water," he said, stifling his giggles. "You should have seen her face." He handed Hannah the cup again, saying, "Here. No tricks, this time."

"Des, that's not smart," Darcy said. "What if it had bit her? And we're in a desert. Danny always said never waste water in this country."

"Poppycock. We'll be at the mine soon enough. You just water the mule."

Hannah drank the water slowly but steadily. Desmond refilled the cup, and she drank again. "Who's Danny?" she asked.

"Danny Comhghall. He's the guy who pretended to be our daddy. The guy who got his head blowed off. The reason you're here."

"He wasn't your father?"

"Nah. He found us in Dallas. We were living in the streets, and he took us in. Said he'd show us the life of Riley, whoever that is. It wasn't bad, neither. We'd go from town to town, staying in the best hotels sometimes, pretending to be rich. Sometimes we'd play like we were poor, just taking whatever we could get. Or every now and then Danny would just let us beg on the streets and he'd run his shell game. And when he'd get arrested, me and Darcy would come in and cry and carry on and beg him to give up his bad ways, scream that Mama was sick, maybe even on her deathbed. And the lawman would, naturally, let him go, and we'd move on to the next town."

"Danny was a bunco artist."

"Yep. He was a crook. But he treated us right.

Never hurt nobody.'' He paused and looked away. ''That was before the gold.''

''What gold?''

Desmond didn't answer. He shouted at his sister to finish with the mule, and stood. Looking down at Hannah, he asked if she needed more water. Hannah shook her head. ''Where did you get the mule, Desmond?'' she asked.

''Stole him.''

She sighed.

''Lady, I won't run the mule as hard as long as you don't try anything. We got a hard climb into the hills. You promise?''

Hannah relented. She held up her wrists, hoping the boy would unlock the handcuffs. But Desmond only smiled. ''Danny Comhghall didn't raise no fool, lady.''

They climbed into the mountains, following a steep and treacherous path slowly and taking frequent rest stops. At dusk, they settled in against the mountain wall. Desmond picketed the mule, and Darcy offered Hannah some jerky and more water. Hannah had decided to bide her time with these two fiends.

She had been spoiled with her orphans. Paco was the wildest one, and he wasn't mean, just a rambunctious boy full of energy who got overly excited and whose voice could fray nerves like chalk on a blackboard. Chris was a hardworking boy who seldom had to be told twice to do anything. Angelica and Cynthia were pleasant girls, though Angelica could be overwrought. Bruce was silent, and Hannah sometimes feared that his brooding would erupt and scar him deeply. But they were good children, loving and kind, who deserved to be loved.

Desmond and Darcy Comhghall, however, were going to be a challenge. Hannah decided that she wouldn't fight them now. She'd let them carry her to the cabin, befriend them, try to make them understand that she could be trusted, that she was here to help them. They were scared. And with good reason. Daniel Comhghall had been murdered. So had Buster Chase.

And if she couldn't make the twins see straight, she'd break free, box their ears, and haul them to Shafter Station. Or maybe she'd be better off heading to Milton Faver's ranch. Don Melitón was a just man, well respected. He'd protect the twins from their tormentors and Hannah from that lynch mob.

Hannah would be patient with the Comhghalls. They didn't know her, weren't used to people who truly cared. Being left on the streets of Dallas, then reared briefly by a confidence man. It would take time to bring those children around. She chewed on the tough jerky and thought about Pete. What had happened? Where was the stagecoach? Was he all right?

She decided she wouldn't be quite as patient.

Chapter Eight

They arrived at the old cabin late the following morning and put the mule in a stone corral common to the area. Whoever had built this place knew what he was doing, Hannah thought. At one end of the corral sat an oblong boulder with a shallow furrow down its center that would hold water for the animals. A well had been constructed next to the well—Hannah wondered how deep they had to go before reaching water—and a wooden sluice led to the corral's makeshift trough.

Twenty yards east stood the cabin made of stones mortared together with mud, with a hard-packed earthen roof. It had been built, she guessed, when this was Apache country, so it looked solid and fireproof. Red-spiked Cardinal Flower, still blooming, and the omnipresent Cane Cholla dominated the yard, and a few pinyon and Texas madrone lined rear of the corral.

Desmond pulled a barlow knife from the packsaddle and sawed away at the rope fastened to the handcuffs. It took a couple of minutes for the dull knife to cut through. Hannah held up her wrists, hoping he would unlock the manacles, but the boy shook his head. "Maybe when we're inside, lady," he said and nodded toward the cabin. Hannah followed Darcy to the

abandoned house, glancing at the boy once she was
out of the corral. He was busy tending to the mule,
and Hannah thought about sprinting away now but dis-
credited the plan. Not still handcuffed. Not before she
had a chance to work with these children.

"Watch your step."

She stopped and turned around. Darcy pointed to a
row of rotted boards that covered a shaft of some kind.
She walked around it to the side of the cabin.
Desmond stopped to pick up a shiny agate, studied it
for a minute, then hurled it toward the well, but it fell
well short of its mark. Sighing, she continued to the
front of the cabin, opened the door, and stepped inside.
Hannah looked back at Desmond, then followed
Darcy.

A hand clamped tightly over her mouth as soon as
she was inside. Hannah struggled in vain. A muscled
arm wrapped around her waist, while the other hand
pulled back her head until her neck hurt. A man whispered to her in a heavily accented voice: "If you
scream, the child dies."

Her blue eyes searched the room and quickly discovered Darcy, already gagged, in the hands of a giant
Mexican. The girl kicked furiously at the buckskin-
clad leviathan who tossed the kid on a dusty bed,
jerked her hands behind her back, and bound them
together with a scarf. Darcy still fought, so her captor
drew a small rope from a coat pocket and tied her feet,
then flung the girl farther on the bed and straightened.
Only then did Hannah realize that the big Mexican
was a woman.

She had shoulder-length black hair streaked with
gray, wore a red silk headband, Apache style, and had

two silver-plated, double-action revolvers tucked in her waistband. She picked up a bolt-action rifle leaning in the corner and looked past Hannah.

"*¿El niño?*" the voice whispered behind Hannah.

The woman walked to a window, peered through the shutter, and replied in rapid Spanish. Hannah only caught a few words, just enough to understand that Desmond was still in the corral.

"I'll release you, madam," the voice told Hannah. "But if you scream, I'll shoot you, then Darcy. Do we understand each other?" The hand loosened just enough for Hannah to nod. He let her go then, and she turned. He was a small but sinewy man wearing dark corduroy pants reinforced with leather in the seat and inside the thighs. A black bolero jacket, trimmed with leather, covered a blue-and-white striped shirt. Around his waist was a belt studded with Mexican conchos and a holster, with six cartridges held in loops on the pouch, tied to his right thigh. His hat was Spanish style, a small flat crown and stiff, flat brim with a leather stampede string tight under his chin.

His face and eyes were dark, his hair coal black, and a small scar stretched from his left nostril to the corner of his mouth. He looked at Hannah's handcuffs curiously. The Mexican woman fired off something else in Spanish. The man drew a strange-looking revolver from the holster and whispered to Hannah, "Go to Darcy. Be quiet. We don't want anyone to be hurt."

Hannah obeyed. The accent was European. Not Greek. Not Spanish or Italian. She sat on the edge of the bed and watched as Desmond jerked open the door, stepped inside, and froze when the man cocked his revolver and leveled the revolver at the boy. "Hello, Des," he said.

Desmond's eyes widened, and he turned to run, but the woman grabbed his pants and tossed him to the floor. She worked the action of the rifle, chambering a round, and aimed at the boy's head. Desmond frowned but didn't move.

The man holstered his revolver. He stuck his fingers in his mouth, seemed to pull his lips apart, and let out a screeching whistle. Minutes later, Hannah heard the pounding of hooves and snorting of horses.

"I am Maksim Yefim," the man said, turning to Hannah. "Originally of Kiev." He bowed slightly, then nodded to the rifle-wielding woman. "This is Paloma. Do not cross her. She has killed forty men and a few women and children." A tall Mexican dressed in black denim and carrying another bolt-action rifle entered. "This," the Russian said, "is Austero."

Austero stared at Yefim briefly, angrily, then opened the shutters to let air and light into the cabin. A shadow crossed Hannah's face and she stared at a man so big he had to crouch to enter the cabin. He even made Paloma look small.

He wore a black sugarloaf sombrero, Mexican-flared pants, and a silk shirt. A machete was sheathed on his left hip, a Colt on his right, with another weapon holstered underneath his left shoulder. Angry, black eyes glared from his dark, menacing face. He looked at Desmond, then Hannah and Darcy, who whimpered through her gag.

"And his," Yefim added with another bow, "is our leader, the hero of Piedras Negras: Plomo."

Plomo slapped his sombrero against his trousers and ran his left hand through his wet, black hair. He looked at the Russian, muttered something in Spanish, and stared at Desmond, who slowly began backing up like a crab toward Hannah and his sister.

"Desmond Comhghall," Yefim said, "where is the gold?"

Hannah flinched when the Russian slapped the boy. Desmond did nothing more than blink, and Yefim sighed and scratched his right earlobe. Plomo's voice boomed out a question. Yefim shook his head and answered in Spanish, then brushed a strand of hair from Desmond's face.

"Des, do you know what it's like in a Russian prison?" He held up his left hand, and Hannah noticed for the first time that two of his fingers were missing. "At the *tyoorma,* they chopped off these to get me to talk. When I didn't, they left me in a cell and told me they'd be back the next morning and would continue relieving me of my digits. I lucked out, though, by escaping that night, fleeing to Sitka just before the Americans took over Alaska."

Yefim snapped his fingers and stretched his right hand behind his head. Austero drew a bowie knife from its sheath and gave the weapon to the Russian, who waved the long, shiny blade under Desmond's nose. "Do you think you could keep quiet if I chopped off one of your fingers? Shall I find out? Or will you tell us what we want to hear?"

Plomo yelled something again impatiently. Yefim smiled. "You know, Des, I believe you wouldn't talk. I think you're as strong as me. But Plomo is not as patient as I am. Those poor souls at Cienega Station can attest to that. We had hoped to take you there, but, alas.'' After signing the cross, the Russian's smile vanished and he stood, staring at Desmond's cowering sister. ''If you don't tell me now, I will kill your sister.''

In three steps, he was at the bed, kicking Hannah out of his way, raising the knife over his head.

''No!''

It was Hannah who screamed. Yefim ignored her, and Desmond sat firm, so she added, ''They don't know where the gold us, but I do!''

Yefim stopped and turned, slowing lowering the knife to his side. Plomo asked something, and Hannah's words were translated. The giant killer stepped in front of her and uttered a long sentence, but his tangy breath was so foul, Hannah couldn't understand even one word.

''Plomo,'' Yefim said, ''does not believe you.''

Hannah held up her handcuffed wrists. ''Why,'' she asked, ''do you think these little devils have me bound like this?'' Yefim translated, and she let the words sink in. ''I came up here with Danny Comhghall, found the gold, and hid it.'' She paused again to think. This was being made up between translations. The Russian finished his Spanish interpretation, and Hannah licked her lips and continued: ''I couldn't bring the gold down with me, so I left, hoping Danny and those kids wouldn't find the gold. I figured I'd come back up and get it, but these twins here caught me.''

Plomo laughed at Yefim's story, and Austero and Paloma laughed with him. Even the Russian smiled.

''Why would that foolish Irishman show you the gold?'' he asked.

"Because." She smiled coyly. "I can be charming."

Yefim laughed and said, to himself, *"Panyatna."* Hannah guessed it was Russian. He was silent for half a minute, then asked in English, "How do you know Comhghall didn't find the gold nuggets?"

Hannah swallowed and started to reply but quickly stopped. Why did he say gold nuggets? Was he trying to trick her? She stalled. "Can I have some water?"

"Austero, *agua.*" The bandit nodded and stepped out of the cabin. Hannah glanced at Desmond and saw him shake his head slightly. His lips mouthed something. A "B"? Hannah wasn't sure.

"The nuggets?" Yefim asked.

"I don't know a thing about nuggets," she said, looking back at the Russian.

He smiled. "Then what?"

"You know exactly what," she said and guessed. "Bullion."

Maksim Yefim tossed the big bowie knife to the table and spoke in rapid Spanish to Plomo. They were still carrying on the conversation when Austero returned with a ladle and let Hannah drink. Hannah managed to pick up a few words—*verdad, oro en barras*—enough to know she had guessed right about the bullion and that they were buying her story. For now.

Yefim turned to Hannah and asked, "How do you know Comhghall did not find the bullion?"

"It wasn't on him when y'all murdered him?"

"We did not murder him, madam."

Hannah shrugged. "Those kids wouldn't have caught me and brought me back here if the gold wasn't still here."

He accepted her story, relayed it to Plomo, and stepped back while the Mexican bandit thought. It didn't take long. He spoke in intimidating Spanish, almost a whisper, and the Russian shook his head sadly and stared at Hannah.

"Plomo asks me to cut off your fingers one at a time until you tell us where the gold is."

Hannah smiled and spread out her fingers. She had expected this. "Go ahead," she said. "But you might as well kill me, and then you'll never find that gold."

"I don't think so. You screamed to keep us from killing the girl. You're not that cold."

"Try me." Hannah's stomach felt like a small boat in rough seas, but her face remained calm. "I screamed because I don't want y'all to get worked up in a bloody frenzy." Did that make sense? She wasn't sure. "I'm not willing to die for that gold, but I'm willing to give it up for my life? Do you understand?" Hannah wasn't sure she understood herself. Yefim looked at her blankly. Hannah swallowed, took a deep breath, and explained:

"I'll walk out of here with one of y'all. Just one. Unarmed! I show him the gold, and I ride out of here while he brings it back to you. You get the gold. I get to live. Savvy?"

Yefim smiled. "And the twins?"

Hannah shrugged. "I don't care about those two."

She waited through the translation. Plomo cracked his knuckles and agreed to her proposal, ordering Austero to follow her to the gold. Frowning, the tall Mexican handed Plomo his rifle and laid his revolvers on the table. Hannah held up her wrists.

"These," she said, "come off. Desmond has the key."

Yefim nodded and searched the boy, found the small key in a pocket, unscrewed the locks, and tossed the handcuffs into the corner. Hannah rubbed her wrists and stood. She ordered the shutters closed and said that if she heard the door or windows open, she'd call off the deal and take her chances running.

"Do not fear," the Russian said. "All we want is the gold. When we have it, we will go. The children will be safe too, if that bothers your conscience."

"It doesn't," Hannah said and stepped outside. Austero followed her and closed the door. He stood waiting, staring at her coldly. Hannah ran her fingers through her blond hair and thought, *Now what do I do?*

Chapter Nine

That morning, after a fitful night, Pete inched his way along the smokehouse wall, feeling each stone, hoping to find a weak spot, crumbling mortar, or moisture. But Cochrane Smith had been right. This building was more citadel than smokehouse. The heavy door was as ironclad as the walls, ceiling, and floor. Belissari and Handal weren't going anywhere.

Pete's stomach felt raw, and for the first time since being shot, he felt hungry. He figured that was a good sign. Until then, the mere thought of food had sickened him. He gently tested the knot on his head, flinching from pain caused by even the slightest touch. Suddenly feeling tired, he found a place in the corner and sat down, leaning against the hard walls, smiling in spite of himself at Merryweather Handal's snores.

The colonel sucked in a rumbling, rattling breath, held his breath, caught himself, and exhaled like a steam whistle. For minutes, Pete stared at the writer in awe. Belissari had known some snorers in his day, but this was unbelievable. Handal noisily inhaled a lungful of air and stopped breathing. Pete waited nervously, started to check on his companion, but the colonel let out a loud breath and shot up into a seated position—wide awake.

"Was I snoring?" Handal asked.

Pete nodded. "I heard Wes Hardin shot a man dead in a hotel for snoring too loud," he said.

Handal laughed. "Just some incompetent scribe's overactive imagination, my friend. Don't believe everything you read—unless it's written by the honorable Colonel L. Merryweather Handal, my friend. I've never had the pleasure of meeting the legendary John Wesley Hardin, so I cannot vouch for the veracity of that legend. Besides, you should not worship men like Hardin. I would never make a hero out of a murderous scoundrel such as he."

Belissari thought about Plomo, the protagonist of two of Handal's dreadfuls. In reality, the bandit was a butcher, feared by Americans and Mexicans alike, but those five-cent novels portrayed him as a righteous man forced to the owlhoot trail by fate and corrupt land agents. Yet Pete said nothing about this. Instead, he just listened to the writer ramble on about justice and heroes and what makes a good story. L. Merryweather Handal was amazing, Pete thought. The man just woke up.

"Now," Handal said, "if you want a hero, I suggest William F. Cody. The best of the bordermen, friend to every decent American man, woman, and child. Showman. Writer. Scout. Marksman. And one of the few men I know whose stomach can hold more John Barleycorn than my own." He winked.

Pete interrupted! "You know Buffalo Bill?" He couldn't help but sound impressed.

"Why, Peter, I count Bill Cody among my best friends—in spite of his friendship with Ned Buntline. I saw him at his Wild West extravaganza in New

Orleans earlier this year. It was raining, so we retired to his quarters and split a couple bottles of rye and talked about old times. Have you had the fortune of seeing his Wild West?''

Pete shook his head.

''A grand affair, Pete. Simply grand. Bill asked for ideas about his show, which I gave him—free of charge, mind you—and we ruminated about old times. He, naturally, apologized for carrying Buntline to national fame instead of me, but I—''

Pete raised his index finger to his lips, and Handal stopped. Belissari listened carefully. The writer stared at him. Slowly Pete climbed to his feet and pressed his ear against the door. There. He had heard something. A horse whinnied nearby.

''Colonel,'' Pete whispered. ''Be quiet. I think we have company.''

''Quiet!'' Handal detonated. ''Why, I'll scream my head off! This is our salvation, man!''

''Or our death,'' Pete replied in an angry whisper. ''If it's Plomo out there.''

''I . . .'' Handal was immediately silent. But it was too late.

''All right!'' a deep voice boomed outside. ''Who's in that shed? Answer me. I got me a shotgun out here!''

Belissari sighed. ''Well,'' he said softly, ''it isn't Plomo.''

Handal took the lead from there. He yelled that they were unarmed, that they were simple travelers who had been waylaid by bandits—twice, no less—and had been left to die and rot in this smokeshed-turned-sepulcher in this dismal piece of desert.

"How do I know y'all ain't deservin' to be locked up?" the man asked.

The colonel told the man outside who they were, promised to give him prominent mention in his next novel if he would be kind enough to shoot the lock off and free them. Belissari waited.

"All right," the man said. "Step away from that door."

Pete and Handal quickly leaned against the wall, book-ending the door. A shot deafened them. The bullet went through the lock and door, ricocheted off the far wall, whining its way over Belissari's head, where it kicked up dust and buzzed past the mustanger's ear while Merryweather screamed and dropped to his knees, covering his head with his arms. The shrilling piece of lead clipped another corner, bounced off the ceiling, and lodged, spent, in the middle of the floor.

Light crept in from the fist-size hole the bullet had punched in the door. The padlock rattled and dropped to the ground, and the door swung in, letting in the blinding sun that caused both prisoners to shield their eyes.

When Pete could finally see, he saw a barrel-chested black man, with curly hair and a massive beard turning white, standing in the doorway, holding a smoking trapdoor Springfield rifle—not a shotgun—in both hands and looking sheepishly at Belissari and Handal.

"Sorry," the man said. "This gun's a mite more powerful than I thought. Y'all all right?"

Both men nodded nervously, the sound of the bouncing bullet still fresh in their minds.

"I'm Napoleon Jefferson," the stranger said.

Napoleon Jefferson was a Seminole-Negro who had

scouted for the Army at Fort Clark. He wore scuffed Cavalry boots, buckskin britches, and a moth-eaten Army blouse missing the regulation brass buttons. His shirt was homespun muslin, sweat and dirt stained his tan slouch hat, and he carried a carpetbag made of such gaudy colors that Pete couldn't imagine anyone carpeting their house with such a fabric—which probably explained why it was used to make luggage.

Jefferson cleaned Pete's wounds with some concoction he carried in a blue bottle. The man's fingers were thick, pockmarked from picking cotton, yet surprisingly gentle. He carefully bandaged the head wound and rubbed salve, from another bottle in the bag, over his torn knuckle. And he did this while L. Merryweather Handal relayed the story of the robbery, crash of the stagecoach, perilous journey to here, seeing Plomo, and being captured by Cochrane Smith.

Handal even quoted again from his Plomo novel: "All along the Rio Grande from the canyons of southern Texas to the badlands of Arizona, the name Plomo—"

"Colonel Handal, sir," Jefferson said softly without stopping testing his wrapping job.

"What is it, my good man?"

"The Rio Grande don't flow into Arizona."

Handal waved his hand. "That's mere geology, Jefferson."

"Geography," Pete corrected.

"It's the story that counts. The action. The adventure. The flow of the writing. Now where was I?"

"I think I might have some boiled eggs and dried beef in that pack mule yonder," Jefferson said, which immediately shut Handal's mouth and sent him trotting to the stone corral.

"Talkative cuss," Jefferson whispered.

"He means well," Pete said. "What brings you this way?"

Belissari quickly learned that Napoleon Jefferson wasn't taciturn himself. He had been born a slave on an Alabama cotton plantation on the Tallapoosa River shortly after the Battle of Horseshoe Bend. Pete wasn't familiar with that history, and it would be months before he discovered the fight occurred in March of 1814, which meant Napoleon Jefferson was seventy-one years old. Pete would have guessed the man's age as fifty.

Sometime during the early 1830s, Napoleon Jefferson fled to Florida and joined the Seminole Indians, who were known for taking in runaway slaves. There he fought briefly alongside the war chief Osceola during the Second Seminole War, but the Indians were defeated and forced to relocate to the Nations like the Cherokees, Creeks, Choctaws, and Chickasaws. Napoleon feared that he would be forced back into slavery. So did many of his new friends, and they fled to Mexico with Chief Wildcat.

Pete was familiar with the rest of Jefferson's story. The Seminole-Negro tribe served the Coahuila government like Rangers, protecting the Mexicans from Comanche and Apache raiders. Then, in 1870, they were recruited by the U.S. Army to become scouts in exchange for food, land and money. Jefferson left his home in Nacimiento and settled near Fort Clark just outside of Brackettville. The scouts never got their land, but Napoleon stayed with the Army in Texas anyway.

Brackettville lay more than two hundred miles east, and Pete had stopped there occasionally on his way home to Corpus Christi. He had even once sold a horse to Lieutenant John Bullis, the officer in charge of the Seminole-Negro scouts. Bullis then gave that chestnut mare to Sergeant John Ward, a scout who had saved the lieutenant's life in 1875.

That thought always filled Pete with pride: A mustang he had caught and broken was now being ridden by a Medal of Honor winner.

"I knows Johnny Ward and I knows that mare," Jefferson informed Pete after Belissari told him the story. "It's a good hoss. Me and you probably saw each other in Brackettville. Small world, I reckon."

Pete nodded.

"Fascinating story," Handal said, wiping egg yolk off his chin with the back of his right hand. "And I can make it even more enthralling, if you'd do me the honor of allowing an interview. With my prose and your experience, you'll be the biggest legend since Daniel Boone. Your likeness, in the finest woodcut, would grace the covers of the latest dime novels. In months, I assure you, you'd be with Buffalo Bill's Wild West. He's talking about a trip to Europe, you know. We'd be rich, man! Think about it."

"I reckon not," Jefferson said, winking at Pete.

Handal sighed and ripped off a mouthful of dried beef.

Jefferson continued his story. With the Indian wars over in Texas, he was out of a scouting job. His wife had been dead some ten years now, his sons were grown and married, and he was restless. "I've always been more doctor than soldier and scout," he said.

"I could guess," Belissari said, nodding at the Springfield. "After your shooting display."

Jefferson laughed. "So I thought I might mosey along to Arizona Territory. With the Apache trouble and all, I figured they might could use a man with my medicinal skills."

"I'm sure the Army is in need of a man with your talents," Handal said.

"Actually," Jefferson said, "I was thinkin' about sidin' with Geronimo."

Belissari was silent. He didn't know if the old man was joking, and if Napoleon really wanted to join the Apaches, it was none of Pete's business. "But," Jefferson said, "I reckon I can at least get y'all two to Shafter. We'd best hurry too, in case them outlaws come back."

They made it La Morita that night, got an early start, and camped on the banks of Cibolo Creek the following evening. Napoleon made Pete ride his saddle mount, a rangy bay stallion with a white forehead. The scout walked in front, leading the horse by the reins, while a panting Merryweather Handal pulled the pack mule.

Much to Handal's displeasure, they skipped breakfast that morning and headed for Shafter. Pete spotted a group of men on the Shafter road, just outside of town. Their horses were tied to a rope stretched between two cottonwoods, and they sat in a circle on boulders, blankets, and saddles, looking grim, rifles close by. Another man stirred a black cauldron, and one stood by the horses smoking a pipe. Pete counted ten men. None of them looked happy.

Handal sniffed the air and said excitedly, "Bean soup, and I'm famished." He picked up his pace, passed Pete and Jefferson, and hurried to the gathering, where the men slowly stood, crushing out cigarettes and emptying coffee cups before picking up their rifles, shotguns, and revolvers. The man by the pot tossed the wooden spoon aside and gripped his pistol butt. The guy at the horses grabbed a shotgun leaning against a tree and rested it on his shoulder.

"Gentlemen, good day," Handal said and laughed. "Sir," he said, looking at the camp cook, "the sight of you stirring that kettle reminds me of the scene with the witches in *Hamlet.*"

"You mean *Macbeth,*" a red-bearded miner said.

Jefferson and Pete followed. The men looked at each other uncertainly. Handal asked if he could help himself to the soup and started to tell about the stagecoach robbery, but Red-Beard cut him off.

"Eat your fill," he said, "then get going. You can make Presidio in a day or two."

"You don't understand," Jefferson said. He pointed to Pete and explained: "This man has been injured. I'm something of a doctor. I'd like to get him to a room in town and examine him more thoroughly. Head wounds are nothing to take lightly."

Red-Beard jacked a shell into his pistol-grip Marlin repeater. "Nobody, and I mean nobody, is going to town," he said.

Chapter Ten

Cholera, the man said. Nobody was coming in, and no one was leaving Shafter until the sickness passed. Some boy had contracted the disease—

Pete didn't need to hear anymore. He swung from the saddle and said, "The Comhghall boy? He's faking."

Red-Beard shoved the rifle barrel hard into Belissari's ribs, pushing him back against the horse. The miner's eyes flared, and Pete realized he had made a mistake. A bad mistake.

"Mister," Red-Beard said, "I've buried my wife and daughter. Nobody's faking anything!"

Belissari apologized, sincerely, and the miner jerked the rifle away with a curse. Pete rubbed the tender spot on his chest, and heard the other men fill in the details.

The Joyner boy had been the first to come down with the sickness, and the cholera, well, it spreads like a grass fire in the summer. Eight people had already died, and now those not sick or caring for the sick were guarding the town, preventing entry and escape. They had sent for a doctor, but the nearest one was at Fort Davis. The mine wasn't operating, and they were all losing money. "Seems like the good Lord's mad at us," one of the men said. Murders. And now this.

Keegan? He had left town before the cholera swept upon them. The deputy was up north with ten men, trying to find the gang that murdered the folks running the stagecoach station at Cienega Station. They had given up Pete and Handal for dead. Some thought that Belissari had even run off with the stagecoach himself.

"You're like Lazarus," a man with a waxed brown mustache said.

"I've been told that before," Pete replied and quickly asked about Hannah. Had she gotten out of town with the twins before the cholera? He braced himself for the worst. Eight, they had said, were already dead.

He wasn't prepared for the answer he received.

Charles Smythe and four men were trying to track down that lady murderess.

The cook explained the death of Buster Chase, the disappearance of Darcy and Desmond, the jailing of Hannah Scott, and her escape. Pete let the story sink in. Napoleon Jefferson pleaded with the men to let him enter town, that he had treated cholera before. Merryweather Handal helped himself to another bowl of bean soup.

"How are the men at Shafter Station?" Pete asked.

"Fine," the cook said. "The cholera ain't spread out of town. 'Course, we ain't lettin' the stages through. Your man Goldman's out tryin' to find a trail around town that's fit for a stagecoach. But you know this country. I reckon y'all are losin' a right smart of money."

Belissari didn't care about the money. He was thinking that he could pick up horses and supplies at the station, find Hannah's trail, and reach her before that posse. Or Plomo. Or Cochrane Smith. He wondered if the twins were with her. One of the men said he guessed Hannah had murdered those kids too. Another one spat out tobacco juice and said, "Not that we'd miss 'em." Pete ignored the laughter. Someone had helped Hannah escape jail. He thought again. Maybe it had been Happy McBride and David Goldman. Maybe she was safe, hidden at the station.

Napoleon Jefferson mounted and, pulling the mule, made his way toward Shafter. Red-Beard cut him off, drawing a bead on the scout's worn-out Army coat.

"I said no one's allowed in town!" Red-Beard said.

"You loco?" another asked. "You ever seen what cholera can do to a body?"

"Get out of my way," Jefferson said firmly. "I tell you I'm a doctor."

Red-Beard let out a mirthless laugh. "You? I wouldn't let you anywhere near my family."

"Your family's dead, Oakley." This came for the pipe smoker, who up until now had not uttered one word. Pete watched the man cradle his shotgun and stare at Jefferson. "Mine's still alive," he said softly. "Or was alive, last I heard. Mister, you sure you know what you're doing?"

"Seen the cholera many a time," he said. "Know all the heathen cures and Christian medicines."

"You could die in there."

"Don't intend to. But I plan on keepin' a lot of other folks from crossin' the river."

Pipe-Smoker nodded and turned to Red-Beard. "Let him in, Oakley."

The miner relented, lowering his rifle and hurrying away, sobbing. Pete felt sorry for the man. Belissari walked to Napoleon's side and offered his hand. The scout's grip was firm.

"Thanks for everything," Pete said.

"You be careful, son," Jefferson said. "You likely got a concussion, and you need plenty of rest." His voice dropped into a whisper. "You ain't rightly fit to be goin' after that gal, the one they say killed that miner."

"What makes you think—"

"I sees it in your eyes. You just be careful, Mister Petros." Jefferson suddenly smiled and straightened in his saddle. "Well, I expect Colonel Handal here will take good care of you."

Pete turned slightly. He hadn't even noticed Handal standing beside him. "You be careful too, my good man," the writer said.

Jefferson nodded, kicked his horse, and, pulling his pack mule, headed into town.

"We're going to Shafter Station," Belissari informed Handal. "You can stay as long as you need, but I'll be taking my leave."

"Bosh," Handal said and shoved a bowl of soup into the horseman's hands. "First you'll eat this. Then we'll walk to your station together. And whatever you plan to do, I shall accompany you. After all, Doctor Jefferson has entrusted your health into my hands, and the honorable Colonel L. Merryweather Handal is a man of his word, a man of duty, and a man in need of adventure and solid material for my next writing endeavors. Now eat, Peter. You'll need your strength. And I shall regale these brave men with our heroic adventures, and see if they have any of Milton Faver's delectable peach brandy here."

* * *

"¡Darnos prisa!" Austero said sharply and shoved Hannah forward. *"¡Pronto! ¡Ande!"*

Hannah got the message. She walked around the cabin and toward the corral, stopping at the covered shaft where she squatted, dug her fingers under one of the boards, and, groaning, tried to lift the piece of rotted timber. Austero grabbed her shoulder and jerked her to the ground.

"¡Queda quieta!" he barked. He bent over, lifted the old wood, and tossed it aside. Austero grunted and threw the next board away. As he bent over, his jacket pulled up, and Hannah saw the revolver shoved in his waistband. They had planned to kill her as soon as she gave Austero the gold. That didn't surprise her. She glanced at the cabin, sprang to her feet, and shoved Austero, jerking the revolver from his pants as the Mexican pitched forward with a slight scream, crashed through the dilapidated boards, and landed with a thud as the remaining timber creaked and fell into the shaft.

Hannah looked at the cabin, thumbed back the revolver's hammer and listened. Surely Plomo and the others had heard the noise. A horse snorted. Hannah tried to think of her next move. The corral! She peered into the shaft, saw no movement from the bandit, turned, and ran. Behind her she heard the shutter fly open, slamming against the wall.

"¡Alto!" a voice cried.

She glanced over her shoulder. Paloma aimed the big rifle, and Hannah quickened her pace, turning sharply left and right like a rabbit trying to escape a coyote. The rifle cracked. The bullet whined past her. Hannah's eyes registered the puff of white rise from the corral, and pain shot through her body even before she recognized the sound of a ricochet.

She was vaguely aware that she was staggering now, not sprinting, and that she no longer held Austero's revolver. Hannah stumbled forward, both hands pressed tightly against her lower left ribs. Each breath caused her to wince, and suddenly she was on her knees, doubling over as if she were about to retch. The ground rushed to meet her, and she instinctively shot out her left hand to brace her fall, keeping her right hand against her abdomen.

It felt like a dream. Hannah pushed herself onto her back, rocking from side to side, and her head dropped to the earth. She lifted herself slightly, saw the bandits running toward her, and forced herself to uncup her right hand. She cringed at the sight of blood, fell back, and sucked in air in spite of the pain.

Paloma stood over her now, scowling. The woman tossed aside her rifle and whipped out a knife. Hannah blinked away tears and gasped when the Mexican dropped on her stomach. She jerked Hannah's head up by the hair and pressed the sharp blade against her throat as Hannah's eyes turned glassy. The last words she heard came from the little Russian, screaming, *"Nyet! Nyet! Nyet!"*

Happy Jack McBride had two saddle horses at Shafter Station, a liver chestnut with a white snip over its nose named Pellizco, and a buckskin named Banana. Both horses were temperamental. Neither was as strong and as fast as Belissari wanted, but they were the only horses available. Pellizco was the toughest, sometimes rowdy, always hard to catch, prone to biting, and angry when tethered. Banana was, more often that not, downright worthless.

"A beautiful horse," Handal said, patting the buckskin's neck. "A fine animal."

"You'll be riding her," Pete said, throwing a sack of corn dodgers over Pellizco's saddle horn.

Belissari had changed clothes at the station, pulling on a relatively clean pair of blue striped trousers and a black-and-white checked shirt. They didn't match, but Pete didn't care. His hat was an open-crowned Stetson some passenger had left behind. Pete Belissari had a big head with a healthy amount of hair, but surprisingly the dun-colored hat fit well enough, though the bandage and bullet wound prevented him from bringing the Stetson down too far on his forehead.

For arms, he outfitted himself with McBride's old 1876 Winchester rifle and a Smith & Wesson New Model #3, just out of the box. Both fired .44–40 loads, which would be convenient. Handal borrowed an old Civil War–era Colt converted to take modern cartridges and a Yellow Boy Winchester '66.

"Dave's tryin' to scout out another road," Happy had informed them shortly after they arrived. "Soon as we found out about Hannah, we sent Felipe to Fort Davis to help out with her kids. And Dave sent off a wire in Marfa to Huntsville for Buddy Pecos. Don't know if he got it, though."

"I appreciate everything, Happy," Pete now said, shoving the rifle in the saddle scabbard.

McBride was a small, leathery man with long gray hair that fell across his shoulders like strings of twine. Apaches had put out his eyes, but the man could judge horses and men better than most. "Wish there was more I could do," he said.

Pete tested the stirrups and bridle again while Handal lauded the blind stationmaster.

"You've done more than your share, Mister McBride." Handal raised the Winchester and Colt over his head. "I assure you, my friend and fan, that when Peter and I track down those nefarious fiends, Cochrane Smith and the bitter Plomo, these patented weapons will become more than tools. They'll become lightning bolts in the hands of the great Greek god Apollo."

Belissari cringed. It was one thing to butcher Shakespeare, to get Alexandre Dumas's heroes mixed up, to misquote or misinterpret other literature, but it was inexcusable, downright sacrilegious, to cite the wrong god in front of a Greek. "Zeus," Pete muttered under his breath, "it's Zeus."

"Do not fear," Handal continued. "For the aim of a righteous man never fails. We'll shoot true, rescue that poor lass from those cutthroats, and send Plomo, Cochrane Smith, and any other brute to meet Saint Peter or, as I expect"—he winked—"to warmer climes."

"Gosh, Colonel Handal," Happy Jack said, "you talk just like you write. It's been an honor to meet you, sir."

Pete shook his head and laughed softly. An hour on the trail, though, he realized that Happy Jack had been serious. For years, Dave Goldman had been reading those silly books to McBride, including L. Merryweather Handal's entire library.

Chapter Eleven

The room smelled of peppermint. When Hannah forced open her eyes she saw Pete Belissari sucking on the piece of candy he had rooted out of the Arbuckles coffee package. Smiling, she closed her eyes and whispered his name. When she looked up again, she realized that the face staring down at her wasn't Pete's.

It was Maksim Yefim's.

He cracked the candy with his teeth and swallowed the bits, grinning at her. "It would have been a waste, my darling, for you to die so needlessly. At least not until we're finished with you." He looked across the room.

She turned her head to follow his gaze, though the effort made her nauseous and burned her lungs. Paloma sat on a stool, her left forehead darkened with a bruise. Plomo sharpened his machete on a whetstone. The twins were tied and gagged, thrown in a corner like dirty laundry. She did not see Austero.

"The bullet ricocheted off the corral and broke two of your ribs," Yefim explained. "Paloma cracked another when she sat on you, and I had to brain her to protect your lovely throat. The bullet bounced off your ribs. You bled a great deal, but the gunshot wound wasn't fatal. However, I feared that you might have punctured a lung. But my doctoring has saved you for now.''

Hannah lifted the blanket covering her. She wore only her petticoat and camisole, the bottom of the latter cut away and turned into the makeshift bandage tightly wound across her lower chest. Anger filled her eyes. ''You!'' Her voice crackled. ''You had the nerve to undress me!''

''Miss Scott,'' he said, ''I think you would prefer my touch to Plomo's. Or Paloma's. And for Austero.'' He crossed himself. ''Well, I fear his fall into the shaft was fatal. He was not moving, and one piece of wood lanced his stomach like a spear.'' He shrugged. ''More gold for us.''

She said, ''If I tell you where it is.'' He stared at her. ''Let the children go, and I'll take you to the gold.''

Yefim smiled and lifted her right hand, which he pressed against his lips. ''Hannah, my dear Hannah.'' He sighed. ''You know nothing of the gold.''

''Yes I do,'' she lied as he released her hand.

He shook his head sadly. ''Hannah, you talked a lot in your delirium. Too much, I'm afraid.''

''You're lying.''

''I'm afraid not. Let's see. Your name is Hannah Scott. You mentioned a Pete quite often.'' He smiled. ''I am quite jealous of him. There are some children, probably better behaved then Desmond and Darcy. You had horrible dreams involving a Buster Chase. And you think the sheriff of Presidio County is . . . well, your words there should not be repeated.

"And, Hannah, you never met Danny Comhghall and never saw his bar of bullion."

She was suddenly parched. "Then why am I alive?"

The Russian brushed hair from her eyes, then waved his mangled hand over her face. "You serve a purpose," he said, and looked at the twins. When he turned back to her, a grim expression had replaced his smile. "I learned many things in that *tyoorma*." His soft voice turned sinister. "You have no knowledge of what we seek or where to find it, but Desmond and Darcy do. I think that when I'm finished with you, after you learn what real pain is really like, when you no longer can scream, when you beg me to kill you, the Comhghalls won't be quite as reticent when I start on them."

Hannah knew it would hurt, but she filled her lungs anyway and spit in Maksim Yefim's face.

They met the man from the Shafter posse at the foothills of the southern Chinatis. He led a lame strawberry roan, said he had just quit Charles Smythe and the group, and was returning to Shafter. Handal explained the situation, told him about the cholera, but the man only shrugged.

He had sandy-colored hair just beginning to turn gray, a pockmarked face, and deep-seated gray eyes. Denim jeans were stuck into stovepipe boots, and a revolver was shoved in his waistband. He wore a blue shirt, canvas suspenders, and a brown hat that looked as if it had been caught in a stampede three or four times.

After making camp, Pete checked the strawberry

roan while Handal fried salt pork in a skillet and the stranger smoked cigarettes, sipped from his canteen, and told his story.

"That Englishman's turned crazy if you ask me," he said. "He's like a jealous husband, bound and determined to find that lady and, if you ask me, string her up. He's offered a five-hundred-dollar reward for her head. Ain't never thought of turnin' bounty hunter for a woman before, but that's a lot of money."

"Where are they?" Handal asked when the pork was done.

The man wolfed down the meat ravenously, answering between swallows. "Here. There. Ain't got a clue where they're goin'. That's why I quit 'em."

Pete slowly rose, patted the roan's neck, and made his way to the campfire. He poured himself a cup of coffee, sat on a rock, and looked at the man.

"Much obliged for the grub," Blue-Jeans said.

Belissari simply nodded.

"How's my horse?" the man asked.

"Threw a shoe," Pete said. "Not much I can do here. You'll just have to take her back to Shafter, though no one's allowed in town."

The stranger nodded, finished his meal, and stood. "I got a better idea," he said, and jerked the pistol from his waist. "I take your horses."

The gun was an old Spiller and Burr .36, its brass frame tarnished green, spots of rust on the black barrel. Belissari wasn't sure if the antique would fire, but he wasn't going to find out.

"By Jove!" Handal shouted. "You'll rob us, leave us afoot in this country after we've fed you? What gall!"

"Shut up!"

Pete hadn't trusted the stranger since noticing his lack of emotion over the cholera epidemic in Shafter. Plus, that strawberry roan had been ridden a good spell after she threw a shoe. Still, Pete sipped his coffee. He'd let this play out, and he wanted more information.

The man laughed. "Funny thing is, folks, that I pretended my horse was lame, told Smythe that I'd have to quit and head back to town. Then that old nag up and goes lame on me for real when I'm scarcely five miles gone." He shook his head.

"What made you quit Smythe?" Pete asked.

" 'Cause I got me a notion. You see, I knowed ol' Danny Comhghall better than some, and I knows he had an old mine up in the mountains. I figure that gal is up there."

"How you figure that?"

" 'Cause them twins is with her. I ain't no great tracker, but I seen some footprints in the cemetery behind the jail. A woman's, and two kids. I didn't tell nobody, though. Because Smythe had offered that reward. I just started thinkin' 'bout where they might have gone. Then it came to me. And I quit 'em."

Pete shook his head. "You're a regular detective."

Blue-Jeans frowned, stretched his arm, and shook the .36 at Belissari. "Don't you rile me none, mister. I'm takin' your horses. Get them hands up. Make a move for your guns, and I'll start blastin'."

Handal's hands shot up. Pete tossed his coffee into the fire and slightly raised his. The man backed his way toward the picketed horses. Banana snorted. Belissari waited. Blue-Jeans glanced at the two horses, decided Pellizco was the better, and moved closer to the liver chestnut. "Easy," the stranger said, but the horse reared and whinnied, fighting the tethers, then swept its head down and bit the man's neck.

Pete moved quickly, drawing the Smith & Wesson and cocking it while rising in one quick motion. Handal still sat frozen, his arms stretched as high as they'd reach, unaware of what was happening. Pellizco whinnied and pounded the earth with his forefeet, while Blue-Jeans grasped his neck with both hands, fell to his knees, and cried out in pain, punctuating every other "Ow'!" with an oath.

The percussion pistol was at the stranger's feet, still cocked, and he looked up at Belissari, pried his right hand from his bleeding neck, and reached for the gun. But Pete stepped up and whipped the long, shiny barrel of the Smith & Wesson across the man's forehead.

When Blue-Jeans awakened, the mustanger pressed the gun barrel against the man's Adam's apple. "Where is this old mine you're talking about?" Pete demanded.

"Don't! Don't! Don't!" the voice shrieked.

The Russian turned from the bed and stared at Darcy Comhghall, pointing his sword cane at the girl. He had removed the gags from the children and smiled at his foresight. "Will you tell me where the gold is, Darcy?" he asked.

The girl nodded. Her brother cursed. "Don't you do it, Darcy! Don't you do it. They'll kill us if you tell!"

"Not if you tell 'em the truth, Des," she said.

"No. I tell you they'll kill us all, even that lady! You keep your mouth shut!"

Yefim nodded and Paloma stuck the gag back in the boy's mouth.

"Show us, Darcy," Yefim said, and added softly in Russian: *"Nye byespakoytyes'*. Don't worry."

Hannah shuddered, though the man had not even begun his torture when Darcy began screaming. She watched as the Mexican woman untied the girl. Her brother kicked and moaned as Darcy walked to the fireplace, reached into the chimney, and slowly pulled away a blackened stone. Her hands disappeared in the hole and withdrew something gleaming. She strained against the weight and dropped the heavy bar onto the hearth, backing away with a slight whimper.

Maksim Yefim, Paloma, Plomo, and even Hannah stared at the beautiful bar of gold.

"Excellent," Yefim whispered, shoving the long, silver blade back into his cane. He walked to the fireplace, patted the girl's head, and said something in Spanish. Paloma turned, threw Darcy on the ground, and had her bound and gagged in minutes.

The three bandits talked quickly in Spanish, their backs to Hannah. She saw the bolt-action rifle near the door and tried to rise, but her lungs burst and she dropped back onto the cot with a groan. Darcy was sobbing.

The Russian turned and removed her gag. "Is this all?"

"Yes," she answered.

"One bar? No more."

"That's all. I swear."

He spoke in Spanish again. Plomo nodded and barked out an order. Yefim walked over to the bed and sat beside Hannah. "You are a beautiful woman,

Hannah," he said, leaned forward, and kissed her. He repulsed her, but she lacked the strength to spit on him again. "I regret what I must do now."

Paloma lifted the bullion in her hands and pried open the cracked door with her left foot. Plomo towered over the children and raised his machete, and Maksim Yefim drew his revolver and placed the barrel against Hannah's temple.

"Good-bye, my love," he said, and a shot rang out.

Hannah jerked, and Yefim rolled off the cot, aiming his revolver at Paloma's back. The Mexican bandit stood straight, blocking the doorway, and the gold bar slipped from her hand and crushed her right foot. The woman made no sound, however. Slowly she turned around, staring blankly. Hannah caught a glimpse of a dark hole over Paloma's right eye before the giant woman fell backward into the yard with a heavy crash.

Another bullet rang, glanced off the gold bar, and ricocheted across the cabin. Plomo yelled something, sheathed his machete, and raced to the door. A third gunshot cracked, and Yefim dived forward, grabbed the gold bar, and pulled it inside as Plomo slammed shut the door, which splintered as another bullet hit.

The two bandits looked at each other in confusion. Then a voice cried out: *"¡Traidor! ¡El deguello! ¡El deguello!"*

"Austero," Yefim said dryly. "The pig lives."

Chapter Twelve

"I knew we should have put a bullet in Austero's head," Yefim said, more to himself than anyone in particular. "Just to make sure he was dead." A shot rang out, and the bullet punched a hole in the door. "He's got that Henry and Sharps we left on the horses. He's got water and food. He can starve us out or hope for a lucky shot."

"Why don't you surrender?" Hannah asked.

The Russian looked at her. "Did you not hear what he said? It's the *deguello*. To the death." The Sharps boomed, the bullet shuddered from the impact, and the heavy lead whined off the wall, shattered the coffee-pot, and lodged in the table.

Yefim swore and stood up. Hannah's eyes widened with fright as he lifted her off the bed and dropped her on the floor in the far corner. She shook with pain and gasped for air. The outlaw then overturned the cot and leaned it against the door. Plomo barked something in Spanish, and Yefim dragged the Comhghall twins beside Hannah, found his place by the side window, and checked Paloma's rifle, slamming the bolt back in place.

Plomo opened his shutter and screamed something, but Austero responded with a laugh and a shot. Angry, the giant Mexican shouldered his rifle and fired quickly, then pulled the shutter close and winced as a bullet kicked dirt into his eyes.

Hannah forced herself to sit, leaning against the wall. She removed the gags from the children and hugged them tightly, reassuring them that everything would be all right. Darcy sobbed, but Desmond complained, asking her to untie him so he could do something.

"I can't, Desmond," she said. "I don't have the strength."

The boy turned his attack on his sister. "I told you they'd kill us if you showed them the hiding place."

Darcy sniffed harder.

"Next time you better listen to me. And what were you doing? That foreign fellow hadn't even hurt this lady yet. You could have at least waited until he done something ugly. You're acting more and more like a girl."

"Desmond," Hannah said. "If you don't shut up, I'll put the gag back in your mouth."

He looked at her and must have seen the hardness in her eyes, for he simply turned in a huff and shook his head. Another bullet pounded the cabin, and Darcy leaned closer against Hannah's aching side. She didn't mind, however. She had won Darcy over. Now she had to work on the boy.

Belissari reined in Pellizco and waited for Handal on the slow-moving Banana to catch up. He took a sip of brackish water from his canteen and studied the rising dust. By the time Handal reached him, he had returned the canteen and pulled out the Winchester, now resting on his lap. He could see the riders, four men on worn-out horses, though he couldn't make out their faces.

"Who are they?" Handal asked as he fumbled, trying to draw his rifle.

"Posse, I expect," Pete replied.

"What if it's Plomo? Or Cochrane Smith?"

"Then you'll get some excellent material for your next masterpiece," Pete said with a smile. It wasn't either outlaw gang. Belissari was sure of that. Plomo and Smith were too smart to treat their horses that way, raise that much dust, or make a charge out in the open. He could pick off all four with his rifle if he wanted, and he wasn't that great of a shot.

"Perhaps I should wait in the rocks," Handal suggested nervously. "That way I could cover you."

"Relax, Colonel. It's the posse from Shafter." The dime novelist sighed heavily and slid his rifle back into the scabbard. Pete, however, kept his handy.

The riders pulled up about ten yards in front of Pete and Handal. Their horses were caked with foamy sweat, heads drooping, chests heaving. Pete spotted blood dripping from a dun's nostrils. He doubted if the gelding would reach Shafter. The men looked equally exhausted, bearded, and dirty. And he could smell them from here.

Charles Smythe's face was sunburned. He whipped off his hat and wiped sweat from his brow, then retrieved a silver flask from his coat and drank greedily. He no longer looked like the English dandy Pete had met in Ulick Keegan's office. His eyes were bloodshot, and his stare seemed vacant.

"How's it going, Mr. Smythe?" Pete asked.

The Englishman looked at him curiously, capped the flask, and slid it into his coat pocket. "Do I know you?" he asked.

"That's Pete Belissari, Mr. Smythe," one of the men said. "The stagecoach man. We thought you was dead."

"Not yet."

"Ah." Smythe smiled. "Yes, of course. You'll be looking for that murdering witch, Hannah Scott." His voice was cold and bitter. The hatred caught Pete off guard.

"Hannah's no killer," Belissari answered.

"She killed Buster Chase!" another man shouted.

"That's right!" Smythe jumped in. "In cold blood! And I expect that she killed Daniel Comhghall too. In fact, this probably was all a bloody plot orchestrated by her—and you!"

Smythe brushed his coattail aside and reached for his revolver. Pete quickly brought the Winchester to his shoulder, levering a round into the chamber and pointing the barrel at the Englishman's chest. Maybe, he thought, he should have let Merryweather Handal hide in the rocks and cover him. This he hadn't expected.

No one else moved. Smythe saw he was beaten and let his pistol slide back into his holster. Pete lowered the rifle, resting the stock on his thigh. "I take it you haven't found her."

"No." Smythe looked away.

"We ain't found nothin'," one miner said. "Been runnin' around the desert like a scared jackrabbit. Worn out our horses. And ourselves."

"We'll find her," Smythe said. "And she'll pay for what she has done."

Handal cleared his throat, and Pete ground his teeth.

"Gentleman," the colonel began, "I am L. Merryweather Handal. Whether Miss Scott killed Mr. Chase or not is a matter best left in the hands of a jury and the Lord. You've done your job searching for her, but I think you have a higher duty to your friends and families in Shafter, and, if I were you, I would make haste and return there."

The mustanger couldn't believe his ears. Handal was brilliant.

"What the Sam Hill is you talkin' about?" a gray-haired man asked.

"It's the cholera," Handal answered. "The ugly plague has hit Shafter. Eight have gone to glory already."

Pete saw the panic in the eyes of every man but Smythe. The three miners talked among themselves anxiously, then one informed the posse leader: "We're callin' in quits, Mr. Smythe. We got family in town."

Smythe said nothing.

The dun staggered forward, followed by the bay and buckskin. The gray-haired man, riding the buckskin, looked back at Smythe and asked, "You comin', Mr. Smythe?" When there was no response, the man kicked his horse into a tired trot and headed to Shafter.

"This isn't over," Smythe informed Belissari when the riders were hundreds of yards away. "I'll go to La Cienega, get a fresh horse and maybe more men. I'll find Hannah, and she'll pay."

Pete's temper flared. "What has she done, Smythe?"

"She killed Buster Chase!"

Belissari responded with an oath.

"I trusted her too, but she ran. She broke out of jail and ran. She made a fool of me. Innocent people do not run."

"She ran from a lynch mob. That's the story I hear."

It was Smythe's turn to curse. He kicked his horse into a slow walk, looked back, and said, "I'll find her. You can swear by it. And when I do, she'll swing from a rope."

"If she hangs, you die," Pete warned.

Smythe laughed, turned around, and rode northeast toward the ranch at La Cienega. Pete could imagine his friend Buddy Pecos telling him, *Up to me, I'd shoot that coyote in the back. Be less trouble that way.* But Belissari could never bring himself to do something like that. Instead, he shoved the Winchester into the scabbard and swung from his horse, leading the chestnut to the rocks. Handal looked at him in bewilderment before following.

"Shouldn't we be moving, my friend?" he asked.

Belissari shook his head. "I want to make sure he is heading to La Cienega first," he said. "I don't want him following us to Comhghall's mine." Pete suddenly shuddered. He had feared for Hannah's safety because of Plomo and Cochrane Smith, and rightfully so, but now it was the deranged Englishman who scared him most.

Darkness came quickly, and Austero's barrage died with the setting sun. Darcy had fallen asleep, her head resting against Hannah's shoulder, but now she awakened as Plomo and Maksim Yefim talked and moved around the bullet-torn cabin. Desmond mumbled something underneath his breath, but Hannah couldn't make out the words.

The two outlaws dared not light a lantern. Instead they waited by the side window, and when the moon set, the Russian carefully unfastened the shutter and slowly opened it. He stared into the blackness outside, nodded at Plomo, pulled himself through the opening, and dropped silently to the ground. Plomo handed him the bolt-action rifle before walking away from the open window, cursing in Spanish and spitting on the floor.

He stopped and stared at Hannah and the children but said nothing. Finally, he turned and went to the door, leaning against the wall, cradling his rifle, waiting.

The night turned cold. The wind moaned. Hannah heard a horse in the corral whinny, an owl hoot, a coyote howl. Or maybe those weren't animals, but Yefim. Or Austero. She waited to hear a rifle crack, but no shot sounded. Not that it mattered. If Yefim killed Austero, then she and the children would be murdered. If Yefim died, then Austero could continue his assault on the cabin, providing he didn't run out of ammunition, and it would be a matter of time before someone caught a bullet. She tried to think of a way out, but couldn't. Her eyes searched the dark room for a weapon, an advantage, a way to trick Plomo. Nothing came to her.

Two hours later, the rifle barked.

Plomo nervously walked to the open window, checked his rifle, and asked in a hoarse voice: ''¿*El*

Ruso? ¿Amigo? ¿Hombre?'' There was no answer, so Plomo asked again. Hannah closed her eyes when she heard a reply.

"Austero están paralizados, mi amigo."

It was Maksim Yefim. Plomo hurried across the cabin, flung the upturned cot across the room, and jerked open the door. The Russian entered, leaned his rifle against the wall, and struck a match. He lit a lantern, found the bullion bar, and placed it on the table.

Plomo said something in Spanish and gestured outside. Yefim scratched his cheek and said, "Paloma? She's too fat for me to move. You do it." He shook his head and said something in Spanish, though Hannah doubted if it was a literal translation of what he had said in English. The Mexican killer frowned but stepped outside. Hannah heard him dragging the dead woman's body toward the shaft.

Yefim glanced at Hannah, then turned his attention to the gold. His frown vanished, however, and he brought the lantern closer, studying the bar closely. *"Nyet,"* he said softly, pleadingly, then whipped out his sword cane and scraped the bullion. The Russian's face grimaced and he swore violently.

Plomo reentered the cabin and thundered over, screaming at Yefim, but the Russian turned savagely and shouted, "It's lead. A bar of lead painted gold! *¡Fraude!*" Yefim was at Desmond in an instant, jerking the boy up by his collar and shoving him to the table.

"Where is the gold, boy?" he shouted. "Tell me the truth." He placed the point of the sword cane against the youth's throat. Darcy sniffed, and Hannah pulled herself up, using the cracks in the stones for leverage. She wavered on her feet, weak, unsure of what to do.

"Tell me!" the Russian screamed.

"There never was any gold bullion!" Desmond yelled. "It's always been a lead bar painted gold."

Yefim blinked.

"Do you think Danny Comhghall would ever live out here if he had a bar of gold? Man, he would have been on the first boat to Europe, spending money like there was no tomorrow. He was a confidence man, you idiot! A bunco artist. He ran crooked shell games and fooled widows into giving him their life savings! He even took y'all in."

Plomo asked for an interpretation.

Yefim lowered his sword and replied slowly, clearly. The giant Mexican stared at the boy, then picked up the bar. Hannah saw the bar, the gold scratched off in several places revealing black. Plomo hurled the bar across the room, where it crashed against the wall and fell heavily to the floor. He spit out orders in rapid Spanish, shoved Desmond back toward Hannah, and stormed outside.

The Russian followed but stopped in the doorway, drew his revolver, and turned around. Hannah stepped in front of the twins, protecting them with her body. Her eyes met the Russian's. His face looked strange from the lantern's eerie glow.

He aimed the pistol at Hannah's chest. She didn't waver, didn't flinch, didn't blink. Finally, Maksim Yefim sighed, slightly lowering and turning the gun barrel, and fired three shots into the cot. Then he stepped outside, closing the door behind him.

Chapter Thirteen

She lost track of time. Plomo and Yefim had taken all of the weapons and animals with them, so Hannah and the twins were stuck up here. Desmond killed a jackrabbit with a slingshot and made a soup, and they discovered staples such as hardtack, jerky, potatoes, and one can of peaches Daniel Comhghall had stored away. With the well, they could stay here for a while. If no one found them soon, they could start walking down the mountain and back to Shafter as soon as Hannah felt strong enough.

It was morning. Hannah stepped outside and felt the sun warm her skin. The outlaws had dumped the bodies of Paloma and Austero in the shaft. Hannah thought it best to cover these up but found that the children had already done so. That troubled her. Throwing stones and dirt over dead bodies was not a chore for two eleven-year-olds. She circled the corral and drew a bucket of water from the well, just to build up her strength, before heading back to the cabin. She met Desmond at the door.

"Where's your sister?" Hannah asked.

The boy shrugged. "She's around somewhere."

He held a blue bottle in his left hand, labeled "Doctor Exciter's Boisson de Vie. The Drink of Life from

Florida. Also cures warts, toothaches, the gout and consumption. Patent Medicine. Guaranteed.''

''Another one of Danny's cons?'' Hannah asked.

The boy shrugged. She took the bottle, uncorked and sniffed it, turned it over, and let the clear liquid puddle in the dirt. ''Come on, Desmond,'' she said. ''We're going to have us a talk.''

She sat on the cot. He shuffled his feet.

''Is this what you plan to do with your life?'' she asked. ''Follow in Danny's footsteps?''

Desmond shrugged. ''It wasn't nothing but creek water, alcohol, and salt, lady. Don't hurt nobody.''

''It's dishonest.''

The boy smiled. He told her he had sold a bottle for two bits to that dumb Joyner boy in town, the one they made watch the lynching before Hannah up and smooth-talked Darcy and changed her ways of thinking. He was bitter about this. They told Joyner if he drank the bottle he'd live forever. It was the fountain of youth that Ponce de Leon searched for. Of course, the simpleton had never heard of Ponce de Leon, so they had to give him a quick history lesson. Then they watched him drink it down straight and only then did they tell him the catch: If he ever lied to anyone, he would die on the spot.

''You ever known a boy who could not fib just a little? You should have seen his face.'' Desmond's laugh abruptly stopped. ''My sister and I had some good times together, and with Danny. But you've taken her away from me.''

''Desmond,'' Hannah said. ''I haven't convinced your sister of anything. She changed her own mind, and you know it. I think she's realized how wrong you both have been. And she doesn't want to live like Danny Comhghall. Or wind up like him.''

''Danny was a good sort.''

''He's dead. You give that some thought.''

The boy sighed and walked to the chimney, reached into the hiding place, and pulled out another blue bottle, which he uncorked and drank. He grimaced, then said, ''It ain't Irish whiskey, but it'll do.''

Hannah let him drink. When he had finished, she asked, ''How did Plomo get involved in this?''

She had to ask him again, raising her voice, to get a reply. ''Danny met a Mexican bandit across the border. Danny showed off the gold bar, and they made a trade. The bullion for a crate of rifles, a dozen horses, and a keg of tequila. Then Danny let the *bandido* share the tequila and got him drunk, replaced the bar with a heavy rock in the Mexican's saddlebag, and got away with the horses, rifles, and fake gold bar. He sold the rifles and horses in El Paso and we came here.''

''He double-crossed Plomo?''

''Well, he didn't know the *bandido* was one of Plomo's men. I reckon Plomo killed the guy when he showed up at camp with a rock instead of a gold bar. The fool.''

''Why not let him have the bar? It's only lead.''

''Danny said that bar was his lucky charm. Besides, he needed it for protection, lady. If he got caught with the bar, he could give it up and hope to get away before they found out it was lead. If he got back safely, he could hide the bar and use it again. Then if he got caught, he could say, no, he didn't have the bar and say that *bandido* had double-crossed his boss, or bring them here, give them the bar, tell him there was plenty more. Make them greedy, so they wouldn't kill him. He could talk his way out of most anything. Danny liked that bar. Sometimes he'd pretend that he was an alchemist and could turn lead bars into gold, then sell the secret formula. You'd be surprised how many idiots there are who'll believe anything.''

Hannah shook her head. She waited for Desmond to look her in the eyes, then asked, "Who killed Buster Chase, Desmond?"

"For all I know, you done it."

She thought about denying this vehemently, changed her mind, and said, "For all I know, it was you."

Desmond smiled appreciatively. "All right, lady. Darcy and I planned this when she ran out of jail. She went to that old coot and told him about the gold bar, said that if he'd adopt us, keep us from having to go back with you, then he could have the bullion. Seemed like a real smart plan to me. We could escape from that fool any time. Only Buster started whipping the tar out of me that night—would have killed me, I expect—then someone come pounding at his door. Buster stopped beating me, opened the door, and I hear him arguing with somebody. Well, I jumped out the window and ran away."

"Who was he arguing with?"

"Don't know."

"Was it a man?"

The boy grinned. "Like I said, it could have been you. Honestly, I couldn't tell if it was a man or woman."

"And do you know who killed Danny?"

"Sure. Cochrane Smith."

Hannah straightened in shock. "Smith? The killer?"

Desmond polished off his patent medicine, burped, and tossed the empty bottle into a corner. "Danny and Smith knew each other a ways back, long before he took us in. Smith stopped us out of town and Danny told us to run. Smith sent a couple of his men after us, but we got away from them two idiots with ease. But old Danny couldn't talk his way out of this one, though I expect he tried his best." The boy shook his head.

The door opened and Darcy came inside. "I'm hungry," she declared.

Desmond frowned. "Why don't you get your new mama to fix you something?" he asked bitterly.

The girl stuck out her tongue. Hannah felt suddenly tired.

Bad dreams haunted her sleep, and when she awoke the next morning she saw Maksim Yefim sitting on her bedside, holding her hand, whispering her name. He had returned. She stifled a scream and jerked away from him, clamping her eyelids closed.

"Hannah," a voice said softly.

Her eyes opened and she caught her breath. Hannah raised her hands to the man's cheek, feeling his beard stubble prick her palms like cactus needles, touching his thick mustache, lips, and nose, finally resting her hands on his shoulder and fingering his long hair.

"Pete?" she said sleepily.

"How do you feel?" Pete Belissari asked.

She sat up and hugged him. He kissed her cheek, rubbed the small of her back, and pulled her closer.

She pushed away, lifted his chin, and stared into his dark eyes, just studying his face, wanting to appreciate every detail, then leaned forward and kissed him.

A man cleared his throat. Hannah looked over Pete's shoulder and saw an odd-looking gent in buckskins. She vaguely recognized him, finally placing him as the passenger who had gotten on the stagecoach back at Shafter Station. That seemed like years ago.

Pete looked at the fellow and stood, saying, "Hannah, I'd like you to meet my friend Colonel Handal."

Her mind was groggy. She still thought this might be a dream. "Handal?" she said, fighting off a yawn. "Like that lousy writer whose stupid novels Paco adores?"

Pete looked away and bit the web between his thumb and finger to stifle a laugh.

The man swept a massive hat from his head and bowed graciously, chattering away, saying something that sounded like, "The honorable Colonel L. Merryweather Handal at your service, madam, noted scribe of the stage and the outstanding literature of the Beadle's Half Dime Library and the Five Cent Wide Awake Library, not to mention one volume of DeWitt's Ten Cent Romances. I have saved your beau from many perils, and he has spoken highly of your beauty, strength, and intelligence. As far as your beauty, though, his words did not do you justice. Alas, no words and no writer could capture that with mere pen and paper."

She was pretty sure she had just been paid a compliment, but . . . she yawned. This had to be a dream.

* * *

After a breakfast of coffee, bacon, and corn dodgers, they shared their stories. Afterward, Hannah and Pete stayed at the table while Handal squatted on the floor and told Darcy about his adventures with the French Foreign Legion, when he had saved a princess much like Darcy from an evil knight and fire-breathing dragon. Desmond, who hadn't felt like eating, walked outside disgusted with them all.

"So what do we do?" Hannah asked.

"We still have Cochrane Smith to worry about," Pete said. "The cholera has hit Shafter. I think the best bet is to get you to Marfa, put you in jail there. Then we'll get this thing cleared up."

"Sheriff Slaughter would just as soon see me hanged, Pete," Hannah argued.

"Maybe, but you won't be lynched in Marfa. They know you there, and Slick Slaughter knows this. Besides, it wouldn't help his reelection if he allowed a woman to be lynched. We'll hire a good lawyer, and as soon as it's safe, I'll go back to Shafter and we'll solve this. Trust me. Outside of Shafter, no one in these parts believes you're a killer."

"Charles Smythe will help us," Hannah suggested.

Belissari frowned. He hadn't told her about the Englishman. "I wouldn't count on that, Hannah," he said. She stared at him, forcing an explanation, which he slowly gave.

Hannah shook her head when he was finished. She started to say something, paused, then began, but a horse squealed and Pete rose from his seat, resting his hand on the butt of his revolver. Hannah looked through the side window and saw the liver chestnut rearing. "Desmond," she said. "I bet he's trying to steal that horse."

Pete ran through the door, followed quickly by Darcy. Hannah rose slowly, protecting her sore ribs, and Handal helped her outside. She saw Pete hurdle the stone fence, watched the horse gallop to the other side of the corral and stop beside a dreary looking buckskin. Belissari dropped out of sight, and Hannah gasped, sure that the horse had kicked Desmond Comhghall.

"Stay back!" the mustanger shouted when Darcy climbed on top of the fence.

"What's the matter with him?" the girl cried.

Hannah and the colonel reached the corral, and the writer placed his right hand on the girl's shoulder, assuring her that everything would be all right. Hannah stared at Pete, who was kneeling over the prone boy. She saw no blood, no obvious wound, but Desmond had vomited and now lay writhing in the dusty, his face pale, pants soiled. Hannah silently cursed herself. She should have known the boy was sick. He had looked pale at breakfast, had refused to eat anything, and as she thought back, she remembered he had not eaten supper the night before.

She walked toward the gate, but Pete stood and shouted, "Stay where you are! All of you!"

Shafter. Hannah remembered now. Everything became clear. When she had been in jail, Mrs. Joyner had stormed in, crying that her Paulie was sick. Paulie was the one Desmond had tricked into guzzling the bottle of Doctor Exciter's Boisson de Vie. Desmond had drunk a bottle just yesterday. What had he said it contained? Alcohol, salt, and creek water. The water, Hannah knew now, had been contaminated.

Cholera!

Chapter Fourteen

The boy's face was cold, his skin wrinkled. He mouthed weakly that he was thirsty. Pete clenched his fists tightly. His knowledge of cholera was limited, but he realized he needed to get Desmond Comhghall to a doctor quickly. Cholera could kill a person in twenty-four hours. "Hannah," he said, "I want you, the girl, and Colonel Handal to stay out of the cabin. Make camp higher up. Don't take anything with you from the cabin, and don't touch anything the boy touched."

Hannah nodded.

"If one of you gets sick, there's some salt in my saddlebag. Mix it with water and force it down."

"What are you going to do?"

"There's a doctor in Shafter," he said. "I'm going to take the boy there. I'll need both horses, but I'll leave the rifles."

He moved quickly then, leaving Desmond on the ground while he saddled Banana and Pellizco. He pulled both Winchesters from the scabbards—they'd only be extra weight—and tossed them to Handal. "Take care of the girls, Colonel," he said. For once, Handal had nothing to say. His head bobbed slightly and he turned away. Belissari left behind the saddle-

118

bags, opting to carry only two canteens and his canvas war bag. He led the horses to the sick boy. He bent and lifted Desmond and eased him into Pellizco's saddle, climbed up behind him and, pulling Banana behind him, attempted a reassuring smile as Hannah opened the gate.

He wondered if he would see her again. For all Belissari knew, in a day he could be dead. Cholera had wiped out Indian villages and wagon trains. Pete tried to tell himself he already wasn't thirsty, that any cramps or chills were just his imagination. He pulled Banana closer, then kicked the chestnut into a high lope, wishing he had a better pair of horses for the task he faced.

Two miles from the cabin, he had to slow the pace as the trail began its descent. Banana snorted and fought at being pulled, and Pellizco didn't like having to carry Pete and the squirming child. Belissari's left hand held the reins to Banana, and he wrapped his arm around Desmond's stomach while he held Pellizco's reins in his right hand. The horse twisted and turned, fighting the bit, but Pete held firm.

Desmond vomited, and the chestnut squealed and danced to its right. The mustanger swore, fighting for control, when Banana accidentally slammed into Pellizco's rump. Belissari heard stones rolling over the edge, bouncing off rocks, and showering the prickly pear some two hundred feet below. The horse regained its footing, and Pete started to look down but thought better of it. He didn't want to know how close they had come to toppling over the precipice.

After that, however, neither horse gave him trouble as they journeyed down the trail; in some places the path stretched no wider than a horse's width. Pete stopped only once on the way off the mountain, adjusting the cinches on both saddles and pouring water into Desmond's mouth. "More," the boy said weakly, and Belissari let him empty the canteen, which he pitched into the rocks.

He shoved the boy back into the saddle and continued. When he reached the bottom, he looked at the vast stretch of broken desert. Desmond groaned and retched violently, and Pete halted again, lowering the boy to the ground to let him do his business. Pete gave both horses a drink from his hat, then realized he had some corn dodgers left in his war bag. He let the horses eat those. The animals would need their strength.

When the horseman and the youth were back in the saddle, Pete patted Pellizco's neck. "Forgive me," he whispered, and kicked the horse's ribs savagely. The chestnut jumped, bucked once, then pounded the desert floor, its ears stretched back, neck pressing forward. Pete kicked harder, wishing he wore boots and spurs instead of the Apache-style moccasins. The wind burned his face and lungs, and the boy, now unconscious, was dead weight in his left arm while Banana almost pulled his right arm from its socket.

The chestnut stumbled, sending Pete and Desmond sailing to the rocky ground. Pete climbed to his knees, dazed, lungs heaving. His right shirtsleeve was torn, his arm bleeding, the bullet wound to his head throbbing again, and he had no idea where his hat had flown, but he found Desmond, still unconscious, and lifted him into his arms, stumbling his way back to a lathered Pellizco. The horse shied from Pete once before he caught the animal, then grabbed Banana's reins and wearily pulled himself back in the saddle.

He kicked and swore, and forced the chestnut into a hard, merciless ride.

Flecks of blood hit his face, and he knew Pellizco had played out. He could hear and feel the horse laboring, but Pete kicked harder, knowing he had to get every inch out of both animals. They crested a hill, and Pete saw a grove of cottonwoods below, an oasis in this country, and forced the animal toward the trees. Beyond the patch of green, the brown and white world continued. When they reached the first cottonwood, Belissari felt Pellizco's front legs buckle.

Pete swung from the saddle, scooping Desmond up in his arms, and was on the ground and pulling Banana before the liver chestnut collapsed onto the ground. Exhausted himself, Pete staggered on ten yards before turning around suddenly and looking back at the horse who had run until its lungs and heart burst. Pellizco's front legs dug into the grass. The horse, its nose coated with blood, tried to raise its head but couldn't.

Pete tossed Comhghall over Banana's saddle like a mailbag and leaned against the buckskin. Belissari's heart pounded his ribs as he unwrapped the canteen around Banana's saddle horn and drank greedily. The horse snorted, and Pete wrapped the reins around his left hand and stepped toward Pellizco.

Belissari pulled the Smith & Wesson from his holster, thumbed back the hammer quickly, and shot the chestnut in the head. Then he struggled aboard Banana and prepared to ride the buckskin to death.

* * *

Darcy Comhghall settled in Merryweather Handal's lap as they sat beside the fire and watched the stars. Hannah smiled as the colonel pointed out constellations and told stories about the heroes the stars were named after. Of course, Hannah had learned enough about Greek mythology from Pete to know Handal didn't have any idea what he was talking about. He simply made things up as he went. It didn't matter. The girl had stopped crying.

Hannah pulled a bag of Arbuckles from the writer's saddlebag, opened it, and dug into the beans until she found the peppermint candy, which she handed to Darcy. Next she wrapped a handful of whole beans in a bandanna, which she dropped in the coffeepot and filled with water from a natural basin. She placed the pot on the fire and waited for the water to boil, leaned back against a boulder, and listened to Handal's tale.

They had made camp about a mile from the cabin in a beautiful patch of desert. The natural basin held rainwater and was full from a recent storm, flowing over into a gully that led to the edge of a cliff. The water fell in a narrow line three hundred feet into another pool below. Texas madrone and pinyon lined their camp, and she had seen the tracks of wolves, javelina, deer, and even a mountain lion, though she knew no animals would visit them with the campfire going.

"And that," Handal said softly, "is the Constellation Falstaff." Hannah couldn't help but giggle. Handal had run out of Greek gods and had turned to Shakespeare. "He's holding his spear and looking at his hunting dog, uh, Banana, and the dog's pointing at a deer. Falstaff was a great hunter."

"Where's the deer?" Darcy asked.

"The deer's not part of the constellation. But Christopher Columbus used Falstaff when he discovered America. You see the tip of Falstaff's spear? It points directly to the Little Dipper, Euless Minor—"

"You mean Ursa Minor. Des told me that."

"Yes. What did I say? How silly of me. Then you know that the tip of the Little Dipper is Poseidon—"

"Polaris."

"Right. The North Star. You can use it to navigate by, which is what Columbus did."

"But, Colonel Handal, that's not the Little Dipper."

"What do you mean, child?"

"Des likes stars. That's how I know about Ursa Minor. Danny taught us to find the Little Dipper. See that star there?"

Handal nodded.

"That's the North Star." The traced a pattern across the sky with her finger. "There's the handle and there's the ladle. That's the Little Dipper."

"By jingo, you're right. What you suppose that little little dipper is then?"

"I don't know."

Handal kissed the top of Darcy's head. "Well," he said, "what if we name it Darcy's Little Dipper?"

"I'd like that," the girl said. She sniffed then, starting to cry again, looked at Hannah pleadingly, and said, "You think your friend can get my brother to that doctor in time?"

"Yes, Darcy. Of course."

"It's a long way."

"Let me tell you about Pete Belissari. How we first met," Hannah said, and she began the story about how the mustanger had shown up in her yard more than a year ago, how he had helped her, how he had been kidnapped and left in the desert to die but had captured a wild mustang and ridden it back to town, entered the horse in a grueling horse race, and won. When she had finished, Darcy was asleep in Handal's arm.

The colonel smiled. "A fine tall tale, Miss Scott," he said.

"It's all true, Colonel Handal."

"Really? Honestly? Hmmmmm. Do you think Pete would allow me to capture his story in the form of a novel?"

"What do you think?"

Handal sighed. "Is the coffee ready?" he asked.

The buckskin fought against being run, but Pete pushed it anyway. He jerked out his revolver, laid the barrel against the horse's rump, and fired so that the powder flash burned the skin. Banana squealed and found an extra burst of speed. When the animal tried to slow again, Belissari pulled the trigger once more.

It was dark now, but he had found the banks of Cibolo Creek and made no attempt to slow down. He pounded the horse's flanks with the pistol barrel, whipped the reins, and kicked the ribs harder. He could make out a fire ahead of him and knew that would be the Shafter guards. Beyond them, he saw another fire burning in town. He didn't want to stop for the Shafter men. That would only waste time, so he put the reins in his mouth and raised the Smith & Wesson.

His left arm pulled Desmond closer. Pete couldn't

tell if the boy was still alive. Banana splashed in the creek, almost slipped, and found his footing on the rocky banks. From the campfire to his left and the glow of moon and stars, he saw several men running toward him, heard their screams.

Pete aimed and fired once, making sure he shot well over their heads. To his surprise, the men scattered like leaves. Belissari jerked the reins hard when he hit the main road, turning at the gallows tree. He heard the report of a rifle, but the shot was well off its mark. Banana stumbled again before continuing into Shafter.

A bonfire raged in the center of the streets, and Pete saw several men adding clothes, furniture, anything to the conflagration. He made out their confused stares in the orange glow from the roaring blaze as he pulled the reins from his mouth and jerked Banana to a sliding stop in front of the fire.

"Where's the doctor?" Pete shouted, gathering Desmond in his arms and sliding from the saddle. His legs buckled when he hit solid ground, and he almost fell. It was like he had forgotten how to walk. He realized no one had answered him, so he fired off the question again, this time adding, "Napoleon Jefferson? The old Seminole-Negro scout? This boy's got the cholera!"

The men backed away from him now. One pointed a finger at a long saloon, and Pete ran across the street and kicked open the door. The sickening smell staggered him, and he saw rows and rows of people on pallets, five or six women hovering over them, and Napoleon Jefferson pouring something down an old man's throat.

"Doc!" Pete screamed. "I got a sick boy on my hands!"

He tried to step forward, but his legs no longer worked, and Pete Belissari crashed headfirst to the floor.

Chapter Fifteen

Hannah woke up with smoke blowing in her face. The remaining chunks of wood were smoldering, and the white smoke slithered low across the ground like a snake and glided across her face. She sat up, wiping sleep from her eyes and soot from her cheeks. On the other side of the campfire she heard L. Merryweather Handal's rumbling snores, drowning out the soft, soothing sound of the small waterfall.

"My word," she said softly. It was a wonder she had been able to sleep at all with that racket.

The sun was beginning to rise, so she threw off her blanket and stoked the fire, feeding the embers a few twigs and straw until flames began to leap. She added another piece of wood and grabbed the blue-enamel pot, sloshing it around to make sure there was enough coffee to heat up.

After yawning and stretching, Hannah pulled back the blanket to check on Darcy Comhghall. She froze momentarily at the saddlebags and coat the blanket had covered. Then Hannah jumped up, her eyes darting across the country, and shouted: "Darcy!"

Handal continued to sleep.

Hannah ran to the edge of the camp, first looking up, then down the mountain. She cried out the child's name again before taking off down the trail toward the cabin. Hannah guessed that Darcy had taken off in the middle of the night, planning to walk all the way to Shafter to find her brother, so she was shocked when she reached the yard to see the girl round the corner of the cabin and start walking back toward her.

Darcy struggled, carrying the lead bar, hunched over and panting. Hannah stopped, perplexed, then walked briskly to the girl, who stopped and let the bar drop into the sand. She looked up at Hannah and waited.

"Darcy!" Hannah shouted. "Didn't you hear what Pete said? Leave that lead bar alone and come with me. You weren't supposed to touch anything in the cabin."

The child glanced at the bar, shrugged, and tried to pick it up. Hannah reached forward, grabbed Darcy's left arm, and jerked her forward. "Leave it!"

"But it's mine!" Darcy started to sob. She was pouting.

"It's only a bar of lead."

"It's mine. I want it."

"We'll get it later. Now let's get back to camp so I can scrub your hands. Did you touch anything else?"

"No, ma'am."

A horse snorted. Hannah swallowed and pulled Darcy behind her. It was too early for Pete to be back. She wished she had brought a Winchester with her. "Darcy," she said, "I want you to run up the hill back to camp. Wake Colonel Handal and stay with him."

"And my bar?"

"I said we'll get it later."

Hannah stared at the cabin and gasped at the sight

of the man who stepped out of the shadows. He was caked with dust and grime, bearded, worn down, with hollow cheeks and vacant eyes. She would not have recognized him if not for his accent.

"Hello, Hannah," Charles Smythe said.

She pushed Darcy away and whispered, "Run, child, run."

Smythe's thumb moved back and forth across the grip of his rifle. He ignored the girl, looking Hannah up and down. His eyes grew harder and his fingers turned white as he gripped the Winchester.

"I didn't kill Buster Chase," Hannah said. "Come with me to our camp, Charles. You look hungry."

Sudden anger masked Smythe's face. He worked the lever of the rifle, swung the barrel around, and fired from the hip. The bullet whined overhead harmlessly and Hannah turned to run as the Englishman swore and cocked the Winchester. Hannah tripped over Darcy and sent herself and the girl, who had never left Hannah, onto the ground.

A bullet kicked dirt into Hannah's eyes. She looked fearfully at Smythe, pulled herself to her knees, and lifted Darcy in her arms. Hannah ran, carrying the girl awkwardly. Another shot rang out, and Hannah dived behind a large brown boulder. She heard Smythe curse and peered from behind the rock.

Smythe worked furiously with his lever, but the mechanism had jammed and he tossed the Winchester angrily aside, reaching for the Colt Lightning on his hip. He stopped and spun around. Hannah heard the horses. About that time, Darcy crawled behind her and looked down the slope.

"Darcy." Hannah pushed her behind the boulder.

"But I want to see," the girl said.

"Be quiet."

Hannah looked around. Four riders had formed a semicircle around Charles Smythe, whose right hand gripped his .38 still in the holster. Two of the riders aimed rifles at the Englishman while a third stretched out his right arm as straight as a railroad cross tie and thumbed back the hammer on his pistol. The fourth man smiled, hooked his left leg over his saddle horn, and began pulling on his reddish brown goatee. Hannah had seen his likeness before, though she could not place him.

"What you shooting at this early in the morn?" the goateed man asked.

"Deer," Smythe lied. "But my rifle jammed."

"You should take care better of weapons," the stringy looking blond rider with the revolver said in a hard German accent. The two other oafs laughed.

The leader looked up toward Hannah, who jerked her head behind the boulder, holding her breath, biting her lower lip, and praying silently as her heart pounded.

"Deer, huh?" the leader said.

"I see it!" another man shouted.

Hannah had shut her eyes. Now she opened them and stared up the mountain. To her surprise, and relief, she saw the fluffy white tail of a deer as it bounded its way over rocks and cactus. She sighed, wet her lips, and cautiously peered below.

"Baker," the leader said, "check the cabin. MacGregor, the corral. Kid Hildebrecht and I will have us a little interview here with this funny-speaking gent. What's your name?"

"Charles Smythe."

"Smith. That's my name. Cochrane Smith. Maybe we're related."

"It's S-m-y-t-h-e. It isn't spelled like some illiterate, illegitimate border ruffian."

Cochrane Smith's right hand left his goatee and drew a short-barreled revolver; he cocked it and fired a round between the Englishman's legs. Charles Smythe, however, didn't jump, blanch, or release his grip on his Colt. The outlaw smiled and commented, "You got sand. I'll give you that."

The rider with the thick gray beard, Baker, came running from the cabin. "I ain't goin' inside!" he said. "There's a sign on the door that says the cholera's been here."

"It is lie," Hildebrecht said.

"Then you go."

The German didn't answer.

Everyone was silent until the puny rider named MacGregor returned. "There's been plenty of people here," he reported. "Been gone a day, is my guess. Except this gent. And he just got here."

"See," the blond gunman said. "No cholera here."

But MacGregor shook his head. "I don't know about that. Looks like somebody got mighty sick in the corral. I ain't risking catching the cholera for even a bar of gold. And like I said, ain't nobody here now." He nodded at Smythe. " 'Cept for him."

"All right, Charles Smythe," Cochrane said. "What are you doing here?"

Smythe sighed. "Looking for the same thing you are," he said, and jerked out his pistol.

It was foolish. The German's revolver cracked

twice, the echoes bouncing off the rocks; Smythe spun around, crumpled, and collapsed. Hannah jerked her head back, unable to breathe, but Darcy tried to look again, so Hannah grabbed the girl, clamping her hand over Darcy's mouth.

"Yes sir," Hannah heard Cochrane say. "The gent had sand."

She didn't move again until the sound of galloping horses had faded away.

Belissari tried to recall how he came to be in the huge bathtub. The soapy water was still warm and felt great, so he relaxed. His head had been rebandaged, and on a stool next to the tub was a set of clean clothes and towel. He forced himself out of the bathwater, dried, and dressed while studying the small room.

Shoved against one adobe wall were a small bed and two trunks; a solid oak wardrobe, revolving bookcase, and pier mirror dominated the other side of the room. Pete walked to the bookcase and examined the collection: Shakespeare, Dryden, Milton, Dickens, Byron, Tennyson, even Cooper. But no Homer. Sighing, he rotated the case and picked up a silver-plated cigar case resting on an unframed photograph. The case was empty, so Pete returned it and studied the picture.

Charles Smythe sat on a bench, decked out like a Texas cowboy from chaps to giant Stetson, brandishing a rifle, knife, and revolver—Pete guessed they were the photographer's props. The picture was remarkably clear. Most photographs he had seen were blurred or poorly reproduced. On the back of the print was an address in Galveston and an inscription in flowing letters:

"March 1882. I'm ready to find my fortune in America."

So Pete was in the Englishman's room. The door swung open, and Pete instinctively reached for a revolver he wasn't carrying. Napoleon Jefferson gave him a weary smile and entered, shutting the door behind him.

"How you feelin'?" the old scout asked.

Belissari shrugged. "Better, I guess."

"Not thirsty? Not cold? No cramps? No vomiting? Nothing out of the ordinary?"

Pete shook his head to each question, then asked, "How's the boy?"

"Worst part is over. I've got him takin' birch syrup and blackberries now. You got him to me right in time, but you come mighty close to killin' yourself in the process."

"I killed two horses," Pete said. "I've never done that before."

"Buckskin's still alive, though I don't know how." That surprised Belissari. Maybe he had misjudged Banana. "You were plumb tuckered out, half-dead, so I brung you here, away from them sick folks," Jefferson continued. "You were just talkin' your head off, makin' no sense. I figured the bath would help, but you went right to sleep as soon as I got you in the hot water. So I left you here, not wantin' to disturb you."

Pete thought for a minute, then said, "Napoleon, I could have drowned."

Jefferson shrugged, finally smiled, and said,

"Hmmmm. Reckon I got more to learn as a doctor." He handed the mustanger a handful of dried red berries.

"Juniper berries," the scout explained. "I want you to chew on these, eight a day. They don't taste bad and will help keep you from catchin' the cholera. Why don't you get some shut-eye here? Townfolks say they don't know when the man who stays here will return."

"I need to get back, Napoleon. I left three people in the mountains who were exposed to the boy."

The black man frowned and pulled a whiskey bottle and leather pouch from his coat pocket. "Here's some more juniper berries, Mr. Petros, plus my blackberry-birch medicine. Give the berries to anyone who ain't sick and the medicine to anyone who is. If the Lord's lookin' after you, maybe them folks you left ain't got the cholera. But you got one problem."

Pete waited.

"Them men waitin' just outside town still ain't lettin' nobody out. Not yet, leastways. And that buckskin you rode in on ain't got the strength to carry you past the creek. 'Course, you is a horseman. You know where to find good mounts." He winked and added, "I gots to get back to my doctorin'," and was gone before Pete could even thank him.

The mustanger stepped out of the Men's Clubhouse and checked the sun, guessing that it was about two in the afternoon. The bonfire still raged as he walked down the street. Everyone ignored him. They were too busy burning everything the sick and dead had owned, trying to rid the town of the disease. Belissari stopped where the boardwalk ended and knelt to tighten the moccasin thong across his right calf.

When he was sure no one was looking, he slipped into the livery stable. He had ridden his first mount to death yesterday. Now he was going to steal his first horse.

In the last stall, he found a dark bay stallion with a blaze on his forehead and short socks on both forefeet. It was a quarter horse, probably with a little Morgan blood, just a tad under fifteen hands. The bay snorted and flattened its ears.

"Good," Pete said, "you have a temper. I like that."

After putting the bridle on the bay, Belissari found a Denver saddle in the livery office and walked back to the stall, threw a blanket and the saddle over the stallion, and tightened the cinch. He led the horse to the livery door. "Wait here," he told the horse and stuck his head through the opening.

Someone cocked a revolver and placed the cold barrel against Belissari's ear.

Chapter Sixteen

"There's a hangin' tree at the creek for horse thieves like you." The Texas twang was unmistakable. So was the face, a mask of scars and powder burns with a battered nose and brown leather patch over the right eye.

Buddy Pecos lowered the hammer of his revolver and, smiling, shoved the Schofield into his holster. Belissari sighed with relief and ducked back inside the livery stable, followed quickly by the tall gunman.

"Am I glad to see you," Pete said. "How'd you get in here? They've got this town nailed shut."

Pecos laughed. "I rode in. Them miners ain't gonna stop me."

"You're not worried about the cholera?"

"Been eatin' so many juniper berries, I think I'm about to grow roots. Now, why don't you tell me what's goin' on here."

So Pete told him, as quickly as he could. Pecos removed his wide-brimmed black hat and ran his fingers through his thinning, brownish gray hair. "Well," Pecos said when Pete was finished. "What's your plan?"

"I was going to gallop through that barricade,

swing by Faver's ranch at La Cienega, and pick up some more mounts, then head back to the mine and find Hannah and the others.''

''And then?''

''This plague has about run its course. I can bring Hannah back here to jail—if not here, to Presidio or Marfa—get a lawyer, and figure out what really happened.''

''There's still Plomo, Cochrane Smith, and that English gent.''

''Plomo's headed back to Mexico. I don't think Cochrane would try anything in town, especially once he finds out there is no gold. The Englishman? I don't know about him.''

Pecos shook his head. ''You should have killed that gent when you had the chance.''

Belissari couldn't help but smile. ''Too late now,'' he said. ''Anyway, Hannah's much safer in town than she is out there, especially now that you're here.''

Pecos fetched a tobacco pouch from his vest pocket and stuffed his cheek with a giant plug. ''All right. As far as I know, I'm still deputized by Slick Slaughter, so that gives me the authority to borrow some other horses from this stable. That'll save us a good chunk of time if we don't have to ride to La Cienega.''

''We still have to get out of town.''

The gunman snorted. ''We rode in. We'll ride out. And I got a Big Fifty if them miners got a problem with that. Now pick out some mounts and one for yourself.''

Belissari nodded at the stallion. ''I'll take this one.''

''No,'' Pecos said with a hard frown. ''That's my

horse. I bought him in Marathon. That's my saddle too. You do got good horse sense.''

Somehow they had managed to bring Charles Smythe to camp, but Hannah never could have done it without Merryweather Handal. She had sent Darcy to fetch the novelist, who practically dragged the Englishman up the mountain. The colonel was gasping for breath and sweating up a storm by the time they reached the site. Smythe, however, was in worse shape.

He had lost a tremendous amount of blood. One bullet had gone through his right abdomen, inches above his waistline and tearing a ragged path, exiting near his hip. The second slug took Smythe in the left shoulder, bounced off the shoulder blade, and glanced downward, lodging just below his armpit. Hannah could feel the bullet. She knew she'd have to cut it out, then cauterize both wounds. Even then, she didn't know if Smythe would live.

''He tried to kill you,'' Darcy said.

''I know.''

''Well, why don't you just let him die?''

''That wouldn't be Christian,'' Hannah said.

''Maybe, but it'd be smart.''

Sighing, Hannah placed the blade of the Englishman's bowie knife in the fire. Smythe mumbled something incoherent. His head was resting on Hannah's bedroll, his face wet with sweat. Hannah tore off his shirt and stretched out his left arm so she could dig out the bullet. She found a pewter flask in the man's trouser pocket and poured a generous amount of whiskey into the shoulder wound. Smythe groaned but remained unconscious.

"Colonel," Hannah said, "I need you to sit on his chest and hold him down. Darcy, I want you to pin down that arm. Don't let him move."

The girl did so immediately. Handal, on the other hand, had to be prodded. Finally, the writer lowered his body on top of the unconscious man. Handal's face was drained of all color, and Hannah thought he might faint. He wavered a bit, then sealed his eyelids shut and said, "Get on with it, ma'am."

Hannah swallowed and pulled the knife from the fire. She felt along the flesh until she found the bullet again, then made a quick incision and returned the blade to the fire. Her fingers were sticky with blood as she probed and gripped the flattened piece of lead, which she pulled out and dropped into the sand. After cleaning the cut with whiskey, she wiped her fingers on her blouse and waited until the blade was white hot. Smythe groaned again, and Hannah removed the knife and, after taking a deep breath, pressed the flat edge of the blade against the shoulder wound.

Smythe's eyes shot open and he screamed, jerking his body despite the efforts of Handal and Darcy. His spasms only lasted a few seconds before he fell still once more.

"Move," Hannah told the colonel, who rolled off Smythe's body and rocked on his knees.

"Are you all right, Mr. Colonel?" Darcy asked.

The writer didn't answer. Hannah splashed more whiskey on the shoulder wound, then washed out the hole in Smythe's abdomen. Again, she heated up the blade and cauterized the wound, first in this abdomen, then the exit hole above his hip, only the Englishman never moved or mumbled. Hannah emptied the flask over the final two wounds and began tearing strips from his shirt to serve as bandages. For once, she wished she had some whiskey to drink.

She was sweating. She hadn't noticed it. Darcy brought a canteen, and Hannah drank, then offered Handal some water. He didn't seem to hear. The colonel's eyes were still shut, and his lips were moving as if he were offering some silent prayer. Hannah turned away and tied the makeshift bandages tightly over Smythe's wounds.

"That was something to see," Darcy said. She pinched her nostrils. "Smells bad, though."

Handal groaned.

"Colonel?" Hannah said softly, "are you all right?"

L. Merryweather Handal nodded and opened his eyes. He stared first at Hannah and the child, then his eyes fell upon the unconscious man. Finally, he saw the bowie knife. Hannah gasped as Handal swayed. His eyes rolled back, and the colonel pitched forward with a thud.

Darcy Comhghall laughed.

Charles Smythe had not regained consciousness when Pete Belissari and Buddy Pecos arrived. They had faced little resistance leaving Shafter—the men parted once Buddy Pecos thumbed back the hammer on his Sharps—and saw no signs of Cochrane Smith on the way up the mountain.

Pecos and Belissari constructed a travois from tree limbs and an old cowhide they found at the corral. It was slow going down the mountain and across the desert. Two days later, they were in Shafter.

Wind scattered the ashes from the giant fires, and the town slowly regained some semblance of life. The barricade was gone, and people were trying to rebuild their lives. A chuck wagon and another wagon full of canned foods, beans, rice, and other supplies were parked near the hanging tree on Cibolo Creek, compliments of Milton Faver. The barber/doctor from Presidio had arrived to help Napoleon Jefferson attend the sick. Presidio's undertaker had also shown up. The whistle blew at the mine, signaling a shift change, when Hannah, Pete, and the others limped into town.

Deputy Ulick Keegan stared at Hannah as they reined up by the hotel. They made eye contact briefly before Keegan looked down at Smythe.

"I'm placing myself in your custody," Hannah said firmly, "after I see to Mr. Smythe and check on Desmond Comhghall."

Keegan nodded and shuffled off toward the jail.

Other than being ten pounds lighter, Desmond had not changed. He sat up in bed and hugged his twin sister, then looked up at Buddy Pecos.

"Who's the troll?" he asked.

"Desmond!" Hannah scolded.

The boy shrugged and asked his sister about the lead bar. "I hid it," she said. Her brother frowned, commenting, "Well, we'll need it."

Hannah felt her fury rising. "Why?" she snapped.

"It's our bar," the boy argued. "We can make a pretty good living with that thing. It's our lucky bar."

"Luck!" Others in the room stared at her, but

Hannah no longer cared. "Danny Comhghall is dead because of that bar. So are a lot of other people."

"It ain't our fault."

She could have slapped him, and she probably would have, but Buddy Pecos surprised everyone by reaching down and jerking the boy from his bed, flinging him over his shoulder and storming out of the room. Desmond screamed in horror. So did his sister, who chased the tall gunman as he quickly made his way down the dusty street.

Hannah, Pete, Handal, and Jefferson slowly followed.

Pecos dropped the boy inside the cemetery, and the frightened Darcy, her eyes filled with tears, could not bring herself to move inside the gate. Desmond tried to crawl away, but Pecos grabbed the boy's shoulders tightly.

"Boy," he said, "my pa would have worn out a passel of switches on my backside if I was a quarter as rotten as you."

"Leave me alone!"

"You got a lesson comin'."

Hannah and the others arrived at the cemetery. She started to open the gate, but stopped. "He'll kill my brother," Darcy cried. "That mean, ugly man will kill Des!" Handal placed his arms gently on the girl's shoulders but said nothing.

Hannah looked at Belissari, then turned back toward Pecos and the brat.

"Let's see," Pecos said. "The fellow who raised you wound up on the wrong end of a scattergun. Some miner was stabbed to death. I never knowed them. But I knew Dick Cody. I hired him to drive that stagecoach. And I was good friends with the Bautistas. They ran a station and raised sheep. Never hurt nobody. But they're dead.''

''It ain't my fault!''

''Says you. And it ain't your fault that my pard Pete almost got his head shot off, that Hannah—who came down here to help you—almost died. Ain't nothing your fault. You think you can play your pal Danny's cons and nobody gets hurt. But how 'bout that lad you sold that concoction to, that drink that almost killed you with the cholera? How 'bout him?''

''Let me go!''

''Open your eyes!'' Pecos thundered. ''Read that tombstone! Now, out loud, or so help me I'll take you to the hangin' tree and string you up!''

''I . . . I . . . can't.''

''Do it!''

Desmond choked out between sobs: '' 'Paulie . . . Joyner . . . 1878–1885. Rest in peace.' ''

''How old does that make him?''

''I don't know.''

''How old?''

''Seven!''

''And next to him! Read that one.''

''I can't.''

''Read it!''

'' 'Maude Joyner. Died of cholera. 1885.' ''

''That's right. His ma. And there's a bunch of other fresh graves here, boy.''

''I didn't know the water was bad! I didn't—''

''No, you didn't. But this is something you're gonna have to carry with you all your days. You and Danny Comhghall come around and play your games and you think nobody gets hurt. Well, everyone pays a price, boy. You want to follow in Danny's bootsteps, go ahead. Somewhere up the road, somebody will be waitin' for you with a shotgun. Maybe your sister too.''

Pecos shoved the boy onto the fresh mound and stormed through the gate. Desmond was bawling now, uncontrollably. So was his sister, whom Handal had lifted up and whose head now rested on the writer's shoulder.

Hannah stepped inside the gate as Desmond scrambled to his feet and ran toward her. She dropped slowly to her knees and was surprised when the eleven-year-old wrapped his arms around her neck and buried his face into her chest, sobbing, wailing, shaking with fear and shame.

"I'm . . . so . . . sorry, Miss Hannah,'' he cried. "I didn't mean to hurt nobody. I didn't want nobody to die.''

Chapter Seventeen

Hannah learned to make the Shafter jail comfortable. Pete and Buddy brought her food, and Deputy Keegan started letting her out of her cell and into his office, where she'd try to teach him the fundamentals of chess. Keegan insisted, however, that Hannah wear handcuffs but he made sure the shackles weren't too tight. Buddy Pecos had wired a man he knew in the Pinkerton Detective Agency for help, and Pete had telegraphed Vernon Kaye in San Antonio to hire the best lawyer he knew and send him to Shafter. Hannah was confident she'd be acquitted if the case ever came to trial, and after the cholera outbreak, she wasn't worried about the gallows tree. The town was too exhausted to form another lynch party.

They were sitting in Keegan's office now, Pete, Pecos, Hannah, Keegan, and Handal. Cochrane Smith had killed Danny Comhghall, and the Cienega Station murders were the handiwork of Plomo. But who stabbed Buster Chase? The deputy opened a desk drawer and pulled out a knife, which he tossed to Pecos. The gunman folded open the lock-back blade, glided his thumb over the blade, and handed the knife to Belissari. It was a small, bone-handled dirk that glinted in the daylight.

"That's the murder weapon," Keegan said. "I ain't never seen it before I pulled it out of Buster's ribs."

"Manasses knife. Too nice a blade for a miner," Pecos commented. "I've taken a few of these off gamblers."

"Well, Buster wasn't no gambler. No one never saw him with a knife like that. He had a rusty old pocketknife that'd barely cut paper, so this sure wasn't his. Which means it belonged to the murderer. So y'all find the owner of that there blade and y'all got the killer. Even I can figure that out."

Handal clapped his hands loudly and exclaimed, "A mystery! I love it. Like Dickens's unfinished *Mystery of Irving Drool.*"

"*Edwin Drood,*" Pete corrected as he turned the knife over in his hand, studying, committing it to memory.

Hannah didn't like the discussion. She couldn't look at the knife. It reminded her of that night when Buster Chase's lifeless body fell on top of her. She still sported a bruise from where the knife handle jammed her stomach.

Belissari closed the blade and returned the knife to Keegan, who dropped it noisily in the open drawer.

"Circuit judge ain't due back for three weeks," the deputy said, "so y'all got that long to find the killer or prepare for the trial. And—"

The door swung open and in walked Napoleon Jefferson. The old scout cleared his throat and searched the room with his eyes. "Them children ain't here?" he asked.

"What kids?" Keegan asked.

"The twins. Desmond and Darcy. I went to check

on the boy in his bed and he was gone. That gal's missin' too.''

A miner's mule had been stolen outside Murchison's Saloon, and Darcy Comhghall had been seen sitting on the boardwalk, chomping down on a stick of candy shortly before the mule disappeared. No one had seen Desmond.

Pete tightened the cinch on Banana's saddle as Pecos led his stallion from the livery. It would be dark soon, but both men had a pretty good idea where the children were headed. Belissari pulled himself into the saddle and waited on his friend, who shoved his Sharps rifle into the scabbard and mounted.

''The old mine,'' Pecos said.

Belissari nodded. ''Makes sense. You heard those kids talking about the lead bar. My guess is they went to get it.''

Buddy snorted and spit a mouthful of tobacco juice into the dirt. ''I had hoped they would finally seen the light.''

They eased their way down the street, only to be stopped in front of the Men's Clubhouse by Merryweather Handal, who had a gun belt slung over his left shoulder and canvas sack in his right hand. The man was panting.

''I figured to come with you boys,'' the writer said.

''Thanks, Colonel,'' Pete said, ''but I'd feel better if you'd stay close to Hannah this time. And see if you can find anyone who recognizes that dirk.''

Handal nodded, but his face showed disappointment. ''Very well,'' he said, ''but make sure that girl is safe. She is a delightful child. Why, while we were in camp, she put on quite a show with a shell game. She had three shells, and she'd put a bean under one of them and move them around and have me try to pick the shell with the hidden bean. Do you know, sir, that I tried fifteen times and not once did I choose correctly? Why, if I'd been betting money, I'd be broker than a cowboy in Dodge City on a Sunday morning. Yes sir. A delightful child.''

''Delightful,'' Pecos mumbled, and kicked his horse forward.

Hannah slowly sat up, rolled her legs off the cot, and stretched, trying to work out the crick in her neck. The morning had a chill to it as she poured water in the basin and splashed her face. Jail wasn't so bad, but she doubted if Ulick Keegan treated most of his guests so well. She heard the door to the office open and turned, expecting to find the deputy with a steaming mug of coffee and an invitation to a chess match. Instead she found Charles Smythe leaning against the door frame.

''Hello, Miss Scott,'' he said. His voice was tired, and he looked pale and weak with baggy trousers held up by suspenders.

''Mr. Smythe,'' she said nervously, trying to look past him to make sure Keegan or somebody was in the marshal's office.

Smythe sighed and stepped toward her, supporting himself with the iron bars. He started to say something, stopped, and cleared his throat as his eyes trained on the dirt floor. Hannah dried her hands on her skirt. ''I suppose,'' Smythe said, still looking down, ''that I owe you my life.''

Hannah remained quiet. She didn't know what to say. There was nothing to say.

Smythe looked up. He tilted his head back, breathed deeply, and stared at Hannah. "I thank you, Miss Scott. I am sorry things between us turned out as they did."

"You tried to kill me, Charles." Her voice was cold.

He nodded. "Yes, but I was angry. I thought I had been played a fool when you escaped from jail."

"I ran from a lynch mob. You would have done the same."

"Perhaps."

A minute passed without words. The door to the marshal's office opened, and Hannah heard Ulick Keegan shuffling around, singing some saloon ditty and stoking the fire in the stove to heat up his coffee. After a few minutes, the deputy stepped into the jail and exclaimed, "Why, Mr. Smythe, you ought not be up and walkin'! You need to be restin'."

"I'm fine, Keegan," he said, "thanks to Miss Scott." He smiled politely and tipped his hat at Hannah before turning around and walking out. He shook hands with Keegan before looking at Hannah again. Hannah still hadn't moved.

"I am sorry," he said. "For everything. Maybe I can make it up to you."

"You can find who owns that knife," Keegan said. Smythe pinched his nose, perplexed, and stared at the deputy.

"Knife?"

"The one I pulled out of ol' Buster. You remember, that folding dirk with the fancy handle. I showed it to you.'' Smythe nodded slightly. ''Well, we figured that if we find out who owns that knife, then we got the killer.''

The Englishman nodded. ''I see. You no longer believe her to be guilty?''

Keegan shook his head. ''Nah, she's too nice a person to go around knifin' men. And she saved your bacon. I don't think she would have done that if she was some cold-blooded killer. So if you want to help her, you go get that Colonel Handal and see if y'all can find the owner of that knife.''

Smythe nodded, pulling his hat down low. ''Keegan,'' he said, sounding suddenly revived, ''I'm sure your name will soon be on the pages of the *Police Gazette*. Good-bye, Hannah.''

Pete and Buddy left their horses in the stone corral and followed the mule tracks past the cabin and up the mountain toward the old camp. Pecos didn't care much for walking but agreed that they had a better time sneaking up on the children by traveling on foot. They found the mule staked and hobbled near the top of the waterfall, at Hannah's old camp, but the Comhghalls were gone.

''Mule thieves,'' Pete said as the animal brayed. ''That's two they've stolen.''

''Hannah's been spoiled,'' Pecos added. The tall gunman knelt to study the small tracks left by Darcy and Desmond. ''These two make Paco look like an angel.''

They heard the twins then, coming down the slope. Pete thought about ducking into the rocks and trees, then realized how foolish it would look to have two grown men hiding from a couple of kids. Instead he stepped beside Pecos, who rose and put his hands on his hips. They waited as the children appeared, talking among themselves excitedly, staring at the ground in front of them. The boy struggled from the weight of the bar, almost entirely black now with all of the gold paint scraped off.

"Uh-oh," Darcy said once she looked up. Both children stopped.

Buddy Pecos hooked the wad of tobacco from his mouth and flicked it over the waterfall. Then he scratched the heel of his right hand against the hammer of his Schofield revolver. The children stared at him nervously before slowly resuming their walk to camp.

They halted five yards in front of the two men. Desmond lowered the bar to the ground and stepped back.

"You two—" Pete began, but the boy cut him off.

"It ain't like you think, mister," he pleaded. "We weren't running away. We just came back to fetch the bar here." He sniffed. "I thought it would make up for everything we done."

Belissari stood bewildered. "What are you talking about?"

"We'd turn in the bar, sell it, and divide the money to everyone who lost someone to that sickness." His head dropped and he choked out the next words: "Like that Paulie boy's family."

Pete's lips trembled as he tried to find the right words, attempted to figure out what the Comhghalls meant. What did they plan to do? Pull another con and give Shafter's destitute the profits? Paulie and Maude Joyner had no survivors, but . . . He shook his head. He wasn't sure if the children were sincere, at first, but tears streaked Desmond's face and his sister was nodding in agreement at everything he said.

Belissari glanced at Buddy, who shook his head, equally confused. The two hadn't tried to run when they spotted Pecos and Belissari. Maybe they were telling the truth.

Pete nodded at the black metal at Desmond's feet. "Son," he said, "I'm not sure what you mean, but a lead bar isn't going to bring in a lot of money."

"But it's not lead!" Darcy cried. Her brother nodded excitedly, adding, "At least, we don't think it is."

Belissari was college-educated, nearing thirty, could read and speak Greek, was fluent in Spanish, and knew some Apache from living out here and Latin that he had learned at the University of Louisville. Yet the only thing he could find to say now was "Huh?"

"It's silver," a voice behind him said, and the mustanger suddenly chilled.

Pete turned slowly and saw a smiling Cochrane Smith, tugging at his goatee with his left hand and waving the short barrel of the British Webley at Belissari's midriff. The outlaw was flanked by his confederates, Baker and MacGregor holding sawed-off shotguns, and Kid Hildebrecht training his Remington on Buddy Pecos's back.

"You two gents," Smith said, "kindly unbuckle your gun belts and toss 'em beyond them rocks."

Both men complied, and the outlaw motioned for them to join the Comhghall twins. Prodded by the advancing gunmen, the prisoners backed up until they were in front of a line of boulders that formed a natural fence. Smith holstered his revolver and knelt by the black bar. He hefted it, smiling, testing its weight, then let it fall at his feet.

"Man," he said, satisfied, "I thought I'd never see this bar again. Desmond, you, Danny, and your sister ran a mighty fine game, but it's all over now." He glanced up at the blond German and casually ordered:

"Kid, kill 'em. Kill 'em all."

Chapter Eighteen

Pete jerked at the loud report only to realize that he hadn't been shot, that the German killer hadn't even pulled his trigger. The mule brayed and kicked, Smith jumped up and swung his revolver around, Baker swore, and MacGregor dived for cover. Kid Hildebrecht staggered backward, lowering the Remington's barrel and clawing at his chest with his left hand. He twisted on his feet like a drunkard while the echoes from the shot trailed off.

Hildebrecht fired once into the dirt and sank to his knees, still turning and instinctively thumbing back the revolver's hammer. Pete saw the splotch of dark red on the front of the German's shirt and a gaping, bloody hole in his back. The Kid pulled the trigger again. He was trying to cock the .45 when he fell on his side, rolled onto his back, and sighed, gripping the smoking gun, mouthing something silently. Hildebrecht was alive, but barely.

"There!" Baker pointed up the ridge.

The entire affair had lasted only seconds. Pete turned to look. He spotted the man on horseback, about two hundred yards up the hill, a rifle aimed in their direction.

"Lower your weapons, my friends, or die!"

Pete tried to place the accent as Cochrane Smith swore and pitched his Webley into the dirt. Baker and MacGregor looked at each other in confusion and tossed their shotguns aside. They didn't have any choice. The marksman up the hill was well beyond pistol or shotgun range.

"Who is he?" MacGregor asked.

"We'll find out soon enough," Smith replied and raised his hands over his head. The stranger kept the rifle trained on them as he kicked his horse and rode into camp.

He was short, with black hair, dressed in a Mexican riding outfit, but he was no Mexican. Pete was sure of that. The man smiled. He carried a bolt-action rifle— Pete had seen only a couple of the old Ward-Burton .50-calibers in his life—into the scabbard and filled his hand with a Lightning revolver.

"Hello, Des," the man said and turned toward the outlaw leader. "And you'd be Cochrane Smith."

The accent was Russian, and Pete realized his rescuer was the cold-blooded Maksim Yefim, Plomo's murderous lieutenant.

Yefim stared at Pecos for a moment, gave Pete glancing consideration, then pointed his revolver toward the lead bar. With his left hand, he deftly opened the saddlebag behind his saddle and nodded at MacGregor. "Kindly load the bar, sir," he ordered.

Thunder rolled to the west and lightning danced in the western sky. Pete hadn't noticed the approaching storm, but the wind picked up immediately, howling, scattering dust and the ashes from the old campfire. Lightning flashed again, followed by a crash of thunder. The storm was moving fast, heading their way.

"Excellent," Yefim said once the black bar was secure in his saddlebag. "This will muffle any gunshots."

"You gonna kill us, mister?" Baker's voice cracked.

"Not all of you." He laughed. "I have only six shots in my Colt, and there are eight of you." He considered Kid Hildebrecht, gasping for breath on the ground. "Seven," Yefim corrected himself. "I need not waste a shot on him."

The Russian dismounted and patted his horse's rear. The claybank trotted off and began drinking from the natural basin. It must have been well trained, Belissari thought. Yefim wasn't worried about the horse bolting because of a gunshot or thunderclap. The killer probably just wanted to be on his feet when he started shooting, not wanting a jumping horse to spoil his aim. The man smiled, reached behind his jacket, and withdrew another double-action revolver with his left hand.

"Fancy finding this here," he said with a wicked grin. "Now I can kill you all."

Baker fell to his knees, begging for his life. He practically had to scream to be heard over the wind. Yefim shook his head and sighed, backing away. Pete stared past him. Belissari had a clear view of the old cabin and mine below, and despite the fading light, he could make out a form below. At first he thought it was a horse, probably Smith's or one of his men's, but he eventually realized there was a man on the mount, a big man on a white horse.

Baker had his eyes shut, Smith and MacGregor stood off to the side, concentrating on Yefim, and the

Russian couldn't pay attention to what was happening below. He cocked both revolvers.

Above the howling wind, Pete asked, "Yefim! Could you tell me what this is all about?"

The Russian considered him briefly. "You know who I am?"

Pete nodded. Baker wailed louder. Smith told him to shut up, and the man's cries became a soft whimper. "Yefim!" Smith sneered. "Where's Plomo?"

The small man with the dark face smiled. "I sent the fat fool back to Mexico. This is a solo venture." Thunder sounded like cannonfire, but there was no hint of rain. "What is your interest in this?" he asked Belissari.

"The twins."

He cocked his head. "Then you probably know how Plomo and I became involved."

Belissari had to hold his hat on with his left hand, but he nodded, forcing himself to look Yefim in the eyes and not stare at the man below and give him away to the Russian killer.

"I came back," Yefim began, "because I started to think about this bar. I wondered why a man like Danny Comhghall would protect it so much, why these children would risk their lives for it, if it was only lead. Lead bars are cheap. And then I realized. This is silver country, and a miner once told me how silver tarnishes, how a film can cover it so that it's blacker than lead. Am I correct?"

He was looking at Cochrane Smith now. Pete took advantage and stared down the mountain.

The man on the white horse was moving uphill now, his horse laboring against the incline, wind, and rider's weight. The wind and thunder would prevent Yefim from hearing him—at least, that's what Belissari hoped. Pete turned quickly toward Pecos, who nodded, having also seen the rider. They'd have to move fast once Yefim realized he wasn't alone.

"So you tell us your story, Mr. Smith," Yefim ordered. "Before you die."

Cochrane Smith put his hands on his hips in defiance and swore, but as he turned to face the Russian he also saw the approaching man. "Very well!" he shouted and stared at the killer. Lightning struck. Close. The mule brayed, and Yefim's horse whinnied, lifting its head and staring at the white horse.

Pete thought the Russian would turn for sure, but he simply told the horse to be quiet and smiled at Smith. "Go on," he ordered.

Many years back, Smith began, he rode with Daniel Comhghall, working odd cons and schemes in places like Fort Griffin, Fort Worth, El Paso, and Tascosa, even as far north as Nebraska. Then they came across the bunco artist in Dodge City who said he was an alchemist and could turn lead into gold. Smith and Comhghall watched him sucker merchant after merchant, so when the gent finally decided to light a shuck south, they followed him. And somewhere in the Indian Nations, Cochrane Smith realized that robbery was a lot easier than thinking up cons. More honest too. So they held up the bunco man and relieved him of his Kansas earnings. His painted wagon was full of six or eight lead bars, and he didn't mind when Comhghall stuck four in his saddlebags. But when Smith found another bar hidden in a chest, the fool pulled out a derringer and forced Smith to shoot him dead.

"We never thought too much about that," Smith said, "bein' young fools' and all."

Smith and Comhghall pulled the cons a couple of times in Texas before they were forced to stash their remaining lead bars under a rock in the Davis Mountains. "There was a posse interested in us by then," he explained, "so we split up. Besides, I was pretty much fed up with bein' a bunco steerer. I headed to El Paso, Danny went to San Antone where his luck ran out and they hauled his carcass to Huntsville. That would have been, oh, '78 or '79, I reckon."

Smith shrugged and continued. He never gave the lead bars much thought until someone explained to him about black silver, and even then he didn't consider it much. He had earned himself a pretty good reputation and was making a fine living robbing stagecoaches, banks, and travelers, rustling stock when needed and cheating at cards. He wasn't interested trying to find some rock in the middle of nowhere for what might or might not be silver.

"Then I heard that ol' Danny was out of prison and pickin' up right where he left off," Smith said. "When I found out he was pullin' that lead-to-gold con, right in my backyard, I started thinkin'. Heard about what he done to poor Plomo too." Smith laughed and continued. "When Danny found out I was lookin' for him, he decided to get out of Shafter, but I was waitin' for him. Trouble was, he wasn't carryin' no lead. Or silver. Or whatever. So I figured, maybe the kids had it. From what I heard, them kids weren't no saints. Anyway, that's the story."

He smiled. "Good-bye, Yefim."

The Russian turned too late to see Plomo crest the hill on his white stallion, screaming in Spanish and waving his machete. Pete didn't wait. He turned, wrapped his right arm around Darcy, and pulled her over the boulders. In the corner of his eye, he saw Pecos tackle Desmond and crash behind the natural fence.

The wind carried away Maksim Yefim's screams. A gunshot exploded. Another answered, and then it sounded like someone had set of a string of firecrackers on the Fourth of July. Darcy tried to look up, but Pete pushed her head into the dirt as a bullet whined off the rock just over his head. He saw his gun belt and revolver, twenty feet away, and began crawling, ordering the girl to stay put.

The wind was roaring by now, and Belissari no longer could differentiate between gunshots and thunder. He lunged the final foot and grabbed the butt of his Smith & Wesson. Rolling onto his back, he slung the holster away, said a brief *táma,* and sat up quickly, cocking the revolver and steadying his right arm with his left, aiming at where he expected to find Smith, Plomo, and the other outlaws. But by the time he was ready to fire, the fight was over.

He paused, looking to his left. About fifteen yards down the row of boulders, Buddy Pecos aimed his Schofield, but the only things standing in camp were the hobbled mule, snorting white stallion, and Yefim's claybank. Between Pete and Pecos sat the children, staring at the scene with wide-open eyes.

Simultaneously, the exclaimed, *"Wow!"*

Chapter Nineteen

L. Merryweather Handal pounded on the door at the Men's Clubhouse and, without waiting for a reply, turned the knob and stepped inside. Charles Smythe glared at him briefly, then finished folding a white shirt and placed it inside a chest. Handal closed the door behind him and looked at the packed boxes.

"You're leaving?" Handal asked.

"Yes," he answered, "and Western hospitality notwithstanding, it is considered quite rude to storm into one's room."

Handal waved his hand. "Excitement on my part. The good deputy informed me that you were interested in helping me find the real killer, so I—"

"You were misinformed. As you can see, I'm leaving town."

Handal considered this for a minute. "But there's a memorial service at the mine tomorrow for those who died of the cholera. I'm sure the people of Shafter would love to have you say a few words. Everyone in town will be there. Well, not Miss Scott."

Smythe shook his head and closed his trunk. "They'll have to get along without me. I think I'll try Idaho. Now, if you don't mind."

Frowning, Handal stepped to the bookcase and

161

pulled out a beautiful leather-bound book. "Dryden," he said. "Didn't he write *Paradise Lost?*"

"No. Good-bye, sir."

Handal returned the book and held up a photograph. He laughed. "What an excellent photograph, Mr. Smythe. You and your cowboy regalia. Sir, a likeness of this could wind up on the cover of my next book. Imagine, with your good looks and my superior writing, this would be money in our banks." He stared at the photo again. His smile suddenly vanished.

"The knife," he said in a whisper.

He bolted for the door. Handal's hand gripped the knob when the blow struck him across the head and felled him to his knees, screaming in agony. Charles Smythe raised the revolver over his head and swung it down viciously, heard the sickening thud, and sank into his bed, gasping for breath.

Smythe waited until his heartbeat and breathing slowed. His shoulder and side throbbed, and he checked the bandages to make sure he had not reopened the wounds. Good. He stared at his revolver and wiped the bloody butt on his trousers. His strength was gone. He'd never be able to move Handal's body from the room, but it didn't matter. Instead, he'd have to leave quickly. He could be safe in Mexico in an hour, but he considered Hannah Scott. Everyone in town would be at the memorial service tomorrow morning at the mine.

"Excellent," Smythe said out loud.

Desmond and Darcy told the story, for they had seen it all. Despite Pete's warning, the girl had sat up quickly to watch the shoot-out. Her brother had done the same. Pete shook his head, which was pounding again, while Buddy walked around camp, checking bodies and weapons. The dark clouds had passed now—the storm had unleashed lightning, wind, and thunder but not a drop of rain—and Belissari listened to the Comhghalls.

Maksim Yefim had screamed when he saw Plomo. He must have shot at the Mexican bandit and missed. By the time Darcy could see, the Russian was staggering back, the machete embedded in his left side, clutching both pistols and firing the one in his left hand blindly.

Plomo leaped from his horse and palmed a revolver. MacGregor dived for Cochrane Smith's pistol and scrambled to his feet. Baker clasped his hands in prayer and continued to beg for his life, but Plomo shot him between the eyes, then turned and shot at MacGregor.

The pistol misfired, and Plomo tossed it aside and jerked another gun from his shoulder holster. MacGregor shot it out of Plomo's hand, so the Mexican yelled and charged. MacGregor, backing up toward the edge of the cliff, pulled the trigger. He screamed and emptied the revolver into the giant Mexican, but Plomo kept running.

Yefim was on his knees, and his pistol, now empty, slipped from the fingers on his left hand, but he raised the Lighting with his right hand and put two rounds into Plomo's massive back. The giant seemed unfazed as he ran forward, wrapped both hands around MacGregor's throat and . . .

Darcy said she blinked. As quick as that, the two

men had vanished. Desmond nodded. "They went over the cliff!" he interjected.

Pecos peered over the side briefly, looked at Pete, and nodded. Belissari let out a long sigh.

"But that ain't the end of it!" Darcy yelled and continued.

Somehow, Kid Hildebrecht managed to sit up. He weakly raised his revolver and shot the Russian in the back. Yefim spun around, gripping the handle of the machete, still buried deep in his side, with his left hand. He fired the Lightning from his hip. The bullet struck the German in the chest and knocked him to the ground. On his back, Hildebrecht raised his revolver and shot Yefim again. That bullet knocked the Russian on his back, and the German cocked the Remington again but never fired.

" 'Cause he was deader than dirt," Desmond said.

Darcy's head nodded excitedly. "And that other fellow fired once, straight up in the air. Then his arm fell to the ground and he was dead too."

Belissari considered the story for a minute, tugging on his mustache before quickly asking, "What about Cochrane Smith?"

"Him?" Desmond said. "Oh, he took off running downhill at the first shot."

Pecos swung around and stared at the cabin below. "You kids stay put," he said, "and I mean it this time." Belissari pulled the bolt-action rifle from Plomo's scabbard and followed his friend down the rugged slope, but Smith was gone. So was Buddy Pecos's stallion.

"Looks like Smith's a pretty good judge of horseflesh too," Pete said, smiling. The gunman turned, his blue eye cold, and his lips turned into a hard scowl.

Belissari led Banana and the horses Smith had left behind back to the camp. "You kids mount up," he said, turning to Pecos.

"I'll straighten up things here, pard," Buddy said. "Catch up with you in town."

The small chain linking the iron handcuffs clinked as Hannah raised her cup and blew the coffee. She stared across the desk in the marshal's office as Keegan concentrated on the chessboard. He had been considering his next move for five minutes now. The door opened, and Charles Smythe entered, taking Hannah's breath. Smythe wore stovepipe boots with spurs, batwing chaps covering his trousers, vest, jacket, shirt, and wide-brimmed Stetson. His gun belt was buckled across his waist. He looked ready to travel. The Englishman paused after Keegan looked up and greeted him before returning his focus on the chess game.

"Did the colonel find you yesterday?" Keegan asked, and picked up a white pawn.

Smythe shook his head and closed the door. "No," he said upon realizing Keegan wasn't looking at him. He walked to the desk, glanced at Hannah, then moved behind the deputy. "I figured you'd be at the memorial service."

"No sir," Keegan said, replacing the pawn with a knight. "Funerals and the like give me the chills. Besides, I got to look after my prisoner."

"I see."

"Colonel Handal said he was gonna fetch you. You sure you ain't seen him?"

"I've been busy."

Hannah placed the coffee cup on the edge of the desk. She didn't like the look in Smythe's eyes. "The rook, Deputy," Smythe said. "Move the rook."

Keegan picked up his surviving bishop. "No," Smythe snapped. "The rook. The piece that looks like a castle."

"Oh, yeah."

Smythe smiled. "Take her knight. That's right. Good."

Keegan leaned back in his chair, satisfied, staring at Hannah with confidence. She used her queen to capture Keegan's rook. "Check," she said.

The deputy swore, scratching his head, and examined the board.

"Sorry," Smythe said. He jerked the revolver from his holster and buried the butt into the back of Keegan's skull. Hannah screamed and dived to the floor as the deputy's head dropped onto the desk, spilling the hand-carved wooden pieces everywhere. Hannah scurried across the floor toward the door, but Smythe caught her, grabbed a handful of hair, jerked up her head, then slammed her into the hard floor.

She groaned and rolled over. Her eyes were slow to focus, but she finally made out the Englishman, straddling her, smiling crookedly. "The gallows tree is all ready, Hannah," he said.

"What?" she asked weakly.

He cursed. "You ruined everything with your meddling! Buster Chase, the fool, told me about the gold bar. I had everything planned, and it would have worked perfectly. You would hang for his murder, I'd kill those idiot children and be rid of this miserable town.''

''You killed Chase?''

''Yes.'' He spat. ''I had to sneak out the window when you came up with that devil of a girl right after I stabbed the fool.'' He laughed. ''Imagine my delight when Keegan locked you up for murder. The lynching would have been perfect. But you escaped, thanks to those twins, and Cochrane Smith stopped me from killing you. That stupid writer is also dead. And now I'll hang you for all that you have wrought!''

''But there is no gold. It's only lead!''

Smythe laughed. ''Ironic, isn't it. All those people died for nothing. And you shall be the last!''

She saw the flash of metal and felt a flash of pain as the gunmetal struck her temple; groaning, she tried to fend off the fog that fell over her.

Charles Smythe rose. He holstered his pistol, walked over to the unconscious deputy, and pulled the body from the desk. Keegan rolled onto the floor. Smythe jerked open the desk drawer, found the Manasses knife, opened the blade, bent over, and stabbed Ulick Keegan in the heart.

It was a precaution. He didn't want to kill the deputy but had no choice—and it really didn't matter anyway. After he hanged Hannah Scott, he'd gallop to the memorial service, saying that Keegan had been murdered, the prisoner lynched, and he was forming a posse. Next, he'd light the fuse to the dynamite he had buried in the Men's Clubhouse. While the posse was forming, the building would explode, burying Handal's lifeless body underneath the rubble. When his body was discovered, they'd figure he was killed in the explosion. In the mayhem, Smythe would scream that it had been Cochrane Smith's gang and he'd go after them alone. An hour or so later, he'd be in Mexico. If they bought his story, fine. If not, it didn't matter, for he'd drift south to Central America and let his father know where to wire his stipend.

A long shot, sure. And if he were caught hanging Hannah, well, Charles Smythe had prepared for that too.

Hannah's head rolled from side to side, then jerked up straight and snapped her awake. She felt something tight against her throat, heard the rippling of water over rocks, and slowly realized she was on a horse, and a rope was tight around her neck. She tried to speak, but the rope was too tight, and she saw Smythe walking behind the blue roan she was sitting on, its reins wrapped around his left hand. He stopped to light a cigar with his right. Her hands remained handcuffed. She glanced up, saw the cottonwood limb, and shook with fear.

The gallows tree.

A horse snorted, and she heard the pounding of metal shoes on the rocks. Hannah's heart pounded as Pete Belissari galloped down the creek bed, jerked Banana to a stop, and leaped from the saddle. "Stop it!" he yelled, drawing his revolver and charging forward on foot. Behind him came the Comhghall twins.

Smythe swore, pulled his Colt, and placed the barrel against the roan's hindquarters. "You stop!" he ordered, and Pete did. "Now toss that pistol in the creek." The Smith & Wesson splashed in the shallow creek, and Pete's hands dropped by his sides.

A crowd drifted from the mine, stopping several yards behind Belissari. There must have been forty or fifty men and women, and Hannah recognized a lot of them. More were coming, looking confused, shocked, but mostly tired. She looked across the creek, saw the two wagons Milton Faver had left, but nobody else.

"What are you doing, Mr. Smythe?" a red-bearded man said.

"Justice!" Smythe answered. "She killed Buster Chase. Leave her to some lawyer, and she'll get off free!"

Someone groaned, and she heard footsteps coming from town. It was Merryweather Handal weaving his way down the dusty road. "No," he said weakly. "No! Don't let him do it!" He stopped by the chuck wagon. His face was bloody and pale.

Smythe cursed angrily. "He can't be alive," he said in a hoarse whisper.

"Smythe!" Handal yelled at the crowd, pointing at the Englishman. "It was Smythe who killed Buster Chase. It was his knife."

A slow rumble rose from the crowd.

"You can't get away with it," Belissari said.

"Sure I can," Smythe said, and he pulled the trigger.

The horse bolted from underneath Hannah.

Chapter Twenty

His moccasins slipped on the smooth rocks in the creek bottom, but Belissari kept his footing as he stormed his way to Hannah. She was kicking wildly, eyes bulging, face turning purple. Only by the grace of God, the rope hadn't broken her neck. He grabbed her feet and lifted her, straining, until he was sure she wouldn't choke to death.

He had a vague recollection of Charles Smythe somehow holding on to the reins of the frightened animal and mounting the horse, of Merryweather Handal charging, and of the crowd from town moving to help. But no one had reached him yet, and he wasn't sure why. Horsehooves pounded the road to town, a gunshot, maybe two, boomed somewhere, and above it all, Pete heard the screaming of men and women. He turned slightly. To his right he saw the colonel, frozen in fear. Behind him he could make out the fleeing forms of Shafter's citizens. Then he smelled the smoke, saw the sparks, and heard the sizzling of a burning fuse.

On the other side of Cibolo Creek, his eyes found the stick of dynamite. The Englishman had mounted the frightened animal, holstered his pistol, pulled the dynamite from his jacket, and touched the fuse with his cigar. He laughed, tossed the explosive to the ground, and galloped toward town.

Pete knew he and Hannah were about to die. If he let her go, she might strangle. He wasn't sure he could reach the stick in time anyway. Stay put and the dynamite would kill them both.

"Don't worry, lad!" It was Colonel Handal. Someone else screamed, and a figure blurred past him. His muscles strained. There was the chop, and he craned his neck to see someone swing a hatchet at the hanging rope tied to the massive cottonwood branch. Across the creek, Handal had picked up the dynamite.

Hannah fell suddenly, and Pete lost his balance and drenched himself in the shallow creek. Hannah lay beside him, gasping, and Belissari scrambled to his feet and saw Desmond and Darcy, the latter holding the hatchet. He jerked them both into the creek beside Hannah and tried to cover them all with his body.

The explosion rocked West Texas, or so it seemed, sending a wave of sand across their bodies. Next came chunks of wood, cans, rocks, everything imaginable. A fist-size rock caught Pete in the small of his back. The rain of debris finally stopped, and Pete rolled off Hannah and the twins. His ears rang. His lower lip was bleeding, and he splashed water across his face, trying to piece together what had happened, still stunned that he was alive.

Later, he would be able to see everything clearly: Desmond and Darcy running past him in the creek, the boy holding the hatchet a miner had dropped. The twins stopping, and the girl climbing onto her brother's shoulders. Desmond handing his sister the hatchet, and her swinging wildly, chopping three times before severing the rope and saving Pete's and Hannah's lives.

But right now, his mind was anything but clear. He glanced at Hannah, who had loosened the hangman's knot and was breathing normally now, though her eyes were glassy and her neck burned from the hemp lariat. The kids sat up, holding their ears. On both sides of Cibolo Creek, men and women began to crawl from their hiding places. Suddenly, Pete remembered and turned and looked across the stream.

Milton Faver's wagons were destroyed, one turned to kindling, the other split in two, one half now on top of an adobe house, the other resting on its side in the brush, one wheel spinning squeakily. The wagon tarps were smoldering, and some of the wood and supplies burned quietly amid the scene of litter. Lying in the middle of the wreckage was the bloody body of L. Merryweather Handal.

"Oh, no!" Pete whispered. He pulled himself painfully to his feet, moved through the water to the bank, and knelt beside the writer's body. Handal opened his eyes. Belissari wiped the red liquid from the colonel's lips and glanced at the man's stomach. The horseman shivered at the sight, looked up, and forced a smile. But he couldn't keep up the facade.

Tears streamed down his face. "Merryweather," he said. "Why? That was a crazy thing to do."

Darcy sobbed behind him. Belissari hadn't heard her follow him. "Don't die, please, Mr. Colonel," the child begged. "Please don't die."

"It's all right, child," Handal said weakly.

Pete looked up. It seemed the entire Shafter crowd now circled the bloody scene.

"Pete." Handal's voice was a dry whisper. "I had to do it." He coughed. "Couldn't let you and Hannah die like that. Remember *A Tale of Two Cities* by Dickens? *'It is a far, far better thing that I do, than I have ever done; it is a far, far better rest that I go to than I have ever known.'* Right?"

Belissari smiled. It was the first literary quotation the honorable Colonel L. Merryweather Handal had ever gotten right. "Fear not, Darcy," Handal said reassuringly. Belissari pressed both hands into the thick red liquid covering the writer's stomach, trying to stanch the flow of blood. Someone behind him sniffled.

Handal closed his eyes and let out a long sigh. Darcy balled her fists and buried them in her eyes, choking out: "No. No. No. No." Pete cried too, unashamed, and covered his face with his bloody hands—but only briefly.

He jerked the hands away and studied them as if they were something foreign. He tested the red substance with his fingers, then slowly brought his hands to his nose. Pete wiped his hands on his trousers and looked at the destroyed chuck wagon. He saw the containers of various vegetables and found what he was looking for: probably a crate of cans, blown apart, labeled TOMATOES.

Belissari ripped open Handal's shirt. Darcy stopped crying. The colonel opened his eyes. "Roll over," Pete barked, and Handal obeyed. Belissari ran his hands up and down the writer's body, but Handal only yelled when he touched his battered head and left ankle. "You don't hurt anywhere else?"

"My head's killing me from where that English

killer pistol-whipped me!'' Handal snapped. ''My ankle feels like it's about to swell up and bust! And I'm
covered with blood. Now let me die in peace, Peter.''

Belissari laughed, picked up a glob of red paste, and
stuck it in Handal's mouth. ''Your ankle's broken,
Colonel, but you're not dying.''

''Indeed,'' Handal said, smacking his lips. ''Tomato
soup!''

Darcy Comhghall yelled excitedly and hugged the
writer so hard that he groaned. Pete left them there
and looked across the creek, where Hannah had been
moved underneath the shade of the gallows tree. Several women were attending her, mumbling things like
''you poor dear,'' ''what a horrible experience,'' and
''the Lord was certainly looking after you today.''
Belissari walked toward her, but the pipe-smoking
miner stopped him.

''Come with me,'' Pipe-Smoker said, and Pete followed him down the road to town, knowing it had to
do with the Englishman.

In the center of the street, he saw Charles Smythe,
spread-eagled, eyes open, clutching the Lightning revolver in his lifeless right hand, bullet hole in the center of his chest. A gathering of men stood staring at
the body, but Pipe-Smoker nodded to another assem-
bly on the boardwalk in front of the long saloon now
serving as a hospital. The men parted for Pete and the
miner, and Belissari saw Napoleon Jefferson, eyes
open and darting, still clutching the trapdoor
Springfield.

''Mr. Petros,'' the old scout said. ''I didn't mean to
do it.''

''He thinks we're gonna lynch him,'' a miner whispered, and another added, "Man, tell him we'll give him a medal."

Belissari stepped onto the boardwalk and took the rifle from Jefferson's trembling hands.

"I yelled at him to stop, Mr. Petros," Jefferson said, "but he kept riding, drew and fired at me. I . . . I . . . I never thought I'd hit him. I shot. But, you remember, I ain't much with rifles and such. I'm a doctor."

"Lucky shot," one man said.

"Lucky for us," replied another.

Pete put his right arm on Jefferson's shoulder. He knew what it was like to kill someone, how it ate at your stomach and heart, the shock of it all, the sickening feeling. You never forgot it. You never wanted to. But you lived with it.

Between Hannah's ribs, Pete's head, and Handal's ankle, no one felt like bouncing around in a stagecoach from Shafter to Wild Rose Pass, so Belissari bought a buckboard and team of horses, and they loaded up for the return home.

The colonel eased his frame into the back of the wagon with the twins, and Handal shook hands with several miners and women who told him, "That was a mighty brave thing you done back at the gallows tree, Colonel," "I can't wait to read your next book, sir," "You're just about as brave a feller as there is," and "Mister, you make Buffalo Bill look like a craven coward." Handal modestly nodded at each compliment and handed out autographs. A couple of miners even offered him whiskey and brandy, and the colonel accepted those too. Graciously, of course.

Buddy Pecos loaded the last piece of luggage, a

heavy satchel, and shook Belissari's hand. "What's that?" Pete asked, nodding at the bag.

"That little piece of metal that caused so much trouble," Pecos replied.

"You have it assayed?"

Buddy shook his head. "Didn't have to. It's what you expected." The gunman sighed. "I got to stay on here for a week or so, till the town council can hire a new marshal."

They shook hands again, then Pete crawled into the driver's seat, released the brake, and pointed the team north to home.

Hannah's ranch never looked so beautiful as it did when Pete pulled into the yard late one evening. The children's dog barked and sniffed before scurrying under the porch and uttering a low growl. "We're strangers," Hannah said with a smile, her still voice a hoarse whisper.

Belissari wrapped the reins around the brake lever and dropped to the ground, admiring his horses in the corral.

"This is it?" Desmond asked. "This is your home?"

"*Our* home," Hannah corrected. She looked back at Handal. "And you can stay as long as you'd like, Colonel." The words strained her raw throat, and she longed for a glass of well water.

Pete patted the left horse's neck and walked toward the cabin. He pursed his lips and scowled. Something was wrong. Where were the children?

The door swung open, and Cochrane Smith stepped outside, smiling, pointing a long-barreled Colt in their direction.

''Welcome home,'' the killer said.

Chapter Twenty-one

"**I** hope you folks were kind enough to bring that silver bar with y'all," Smith said.

"Where are my children?" Hannah shot out, ignoring the dry pain in her throat.

"Take it easy, lady. They're all tied up inside. Them station hands you got is bound and gagged in the barn over yonder. Ain't nobody hurt, 'cept for a headache maybe, and nobody's got to get hurt—if you all is smart."

"Considerate of you." Her gravelly voice punctuated the bitterness.

Smith laughed. "Didn't want to risk a shot. That's why nobody's dead. And your beau here can tell you that I don't use knives for personal, professional reasons. But if you ain't got that silver bar . . ." His smile faded.

"It's in the back of the wagon," Pete said.

"Good." The outlaw nodded at the corral. "One of you bring me the silver, one of you saddle me a horse. I like that blood bay. Looks like a fast runner."

Pete nodded at Hannah, who climbed down from the wagon and walked to the corral. Belissari moved to the back of the wagon and picked up the canvas satchel.

"Don't try nothin'!" Smith yelled at Hannah, who didn't bother to turn around. The killer turned his attention to Pete, who didn't move until Hannah ducked inside the corral. Smith said something, waving the Colt in Pete's direction. Slowly he walked until he was face-to-face with the smiling outlaw.

"Good," Smith said. "Now put the bag down and step back to the wagon with them others."

Pete's eyes shot toward Hannah, and Smith followed his gaze. Just like that, Belissari dropped the bag onto the outlaw's foot. Smith screamed in pain, and Pete's right hand gripped the revolver and forced down the barrel. The gunshot exploded. Pete slammed the killer's gunhand against a hitching rail, and the Colt toppled into the dust. Then Belissari's left fist shot up and caught Smith in the jaw, and both men toppled into the dirt.

Belissari rose first, but the outlaw arched his back and kicked out with both feet, his hard heels slamming into the horseman's chest. The blow knocked Pete against the cedar rail. Belissari rolled, avoiding Smith's attacking boots, and collapsed into the dust. His eyes burned from rising dust and pain. The horses snorted and pulled in their traces. Merryweather Handal and the twins shouted something, but Pete couldn't understand. He spit sand from his mouth and climbed to his knees, blinking rapidly while trying to find his prey.

Smith had pulled himself to his knees. The murderer bent over and gripped the revolver's butt. Pete's eyes darted. He saw the satchel, grabbed it with both hands, and swung it as hard as he could just as Smith straightened, brought the Colt level, and cocked the hammer.

The heavy bag slammed into Smith's face. The pistol barked. Pete felt hot air burn his neck as he toppled backward. When he opened his eyes, Hannah knelt over him, smiling, helping him sit up. Cochrane Smith lay on the ground, moaning, his bloody nose flattened by the lead bar.

"You mean it's only lead?" Desmond Comhghall asked.

"Yes sir," the clerk at the Fort Davis Assayer's Office replied.

Frowning, Desmond and Darcy slowly stepped outside and sat on the boardwalk, heads buried in their hands.

Hannah thanked the clerk and followed the twins. They had refused to believe Pete when he told them the bar was only lead. So now, a week and a half after Cochrane Smith had been hauled off to the Marfa jail, they brought the Comhghalls into town to say goodbye to L. Merryweather Handal and find out the truth. The clerk, a timid-looking man in a houndstooth sack suit and gold-rimmed spectacles, had confirmed the value of the twins' black bar.

"You can polish it all you want," the clerk had said. "But it won't help. This isn't silver."

Buddy and Pete leaned against the buckboard in front of the children. Hannah sat beside them, put her arms around both, and said, "I'm sorry, children."

"But . . . but Danny told us it was silver," Desmond moaned.

Hannah dropped her head, trying to think of the right words. She looked up after a minute and said, "Danny Comhghall was a crook. He was a liar and a cheat. It shouldn't come as a surprise that he lied to you.''

Her throat remained tender from the hangman's noose, but she no longer spoke in a whisper.

''But—'' the children began.

''You said it yourself, Desmond, back when we were at the cabin being held by Plomo. Remember? You told the Russian that if the bar were gold, 'Danny Comhghall would have been on the first boat to Europe, spending money like there was no tomorrow.' He would have done the same if it had been silver. Wouldn't he?''

''I reckon,'' Desmond said. ''Yes, ma'am,'' his sister agreed.

The boy sniffed. ''Now what will I do? I was going to help all them people in Shafter.''

Buddy Pecos cleared his throat. He dropped to a knee and put a callused right hand on the lad's shoulder. Desmond's eyes were wide with fright. So were his sister's. They were scared to death of Buddy Pecos—but then, so were a lot of adults in this part of the country.

''Son,'' the Texan began, ''you learn from your mistakes. Money? That ain't gonna help ease them folks' pain none, won't bring nobody back. What you did was wrong. Bad wrong. But it's over and done with now.''

''But eight people died from the cholera. And all those others killed by Plomo, Smith, that English fellow.''

Pecos shook his head. ''You almost died your ownself. Cholera happens. You didn't know the water was bad. As for them others, I guess justice has been

served. Plomo and his men are dead. So is the Englishman. Cochrane Smith's gang was wiped out, and
he'll be stretchin' a rope before long.''

Buddy paused, thinking for a minute, then resumed.
''Desmond, I done some mighty mean things in my
day. Rode against the law. Was rotten to the core.
Well, now I've realized my mistakes. Don't help me
sleep at night, knowin' all I done, but I figure if I live
the rest of my life right, do good for a change, then
it'll help even out the slate. That's what you got to do.
And, Lord willin', you'll spend a lot more years ridin'
with the law than I'll be able to do. It's over. Ride on.
Don't look back, but don't ever forget what's behind
you.''

He squeezed the boy's shoulder and rose. Pete nodded in approval. Hannah stared, dumbfounded. She
had never heard Buddy Pecos talk so much.

''Hello, friends!'' L. Merryweather Handal, resplen-
dent in his new buckskins and massive white hat, hobbled his way down the boardwalk. He wore one high
black boot, polished to perfection, while his other foot
remained covered in white plaster, clunking along.
Handal leaned his crutch against the adobe wall of the
assayer's office.

Hannah rose and hugged the writer. Handal removed his hat, revealing his bandaged head, and
smiled. ''The stagecoach leaves in twenty minutes,''
he said. ''I was hoping I would be able to treat my
favorite West Texans to ice cream. I have convinced
the good man at your fine bakery to churn up some
ice cream on this glorious fall day. It feels almost like
summer.''

It isn't hot at all, Hannah thought. Handal winked

at her, understanding. "Of course, a little peach brandy poured over vanilla ice cream would be quite a treat for us adults."

She laughed. She couldn't help herself.

"Won't you stay with us?" Darcy pleaded.

The writer frowned. "Alas, child, I can't. I have offers galore from the publishing houses in New York. Many of them want me to write an account of my adventures, how I helped capture the vicious Plomo and Smith gangs and sent them to doom and destruction. *Harper's Weekly* wired to say they'd like to serialize my frontier memoirs, and *Frank Leslie's Illustrated* wants to sponsor a lecture series in the spring. Quite naturally, Beadle's and the Five Cent Wide Awake Library want me back. The nation demands my writing skills, and I must not let America down. Now, how about some ice cream?"

He took Darcy's small hand in his left and led her down the boardwalk, followed by her brother. Hannah looked at Pete and Pecos. Both men shrugged. She ran fingers over her chaffed neck. Brandy, she thought, might feel good, might help her throat. But first she grabbed Buddy's left hand and squeezed it.

"That was nice," she told him, "what you told Desmond. You can be an amazing man, Buddy Pecos. I think we need to find you a girlfriend."

The tall sharpshooter studied her briefly, not smiling, not frowning, probably not understanding. He shook his head, confounded, and strode down the boardwalk after the twins and Handal.

Pete stepped beside Hannah and put his arms around her shoulder. Her eyes danced as she looked at him and said softly, "You're a pretty amazing man yourself, Petros Belissari."

He smiled and whispered, "But I have a girlfriend."

His arm fell at her side, and their fingers locked. They walked down the boardwalk toward Buehler's Bakery. Her ribs still hurt. His head throbbed. Despite more than a week of rest at the ranch, both felt exhausted. But as they continued strolling through town, hearing the laughter of the twins and L. Merryweather Handal's booming voice, Pete Belissari and Hannah Scott felt content.

And, for the first time in weeks, safe and happy.